BABYMOUSE AND FRIENDS*

*...OR ENEMIES!

I THINK THIS
IS MY FAVORITE
ONE YET!

Be sure to read
ALL the **BABYMOUSE** books:

#1 BABYMOUSE: Queen of the World!
#2 BABYMOUSE: Our Hero
#3 BABYMOUSE: Beach Babe
#4 BABYMOUSE: Rock Star
#5 BABYMOUSE: Heartbreaker
#6 CAMP BABYMOUSE
#7 BABYMOUSE: Skater Girl
#8 BABYMOUSE: Puppy Love
#9 BABYMOUSE: Monster Mash
#10 BABYMOUSE: The Musical
#11 BABYMOUSE: Dragonslayer
#12 BABYMOUSE: Burns Rubber
#13 BABYMOUSE: Cupcake Tycoon
#14 BABYMOUSE: Mad Scientist
#15 A Very BABYMOUSE Christmas
#16 BABYMOUSE for President
#17 Extreme BABYMOUSE
#18 Happy Birthday, BABYMOUSE

BABYMOUSE
CUPCAKE TYCOON

BY JENNIFER L. HOLM & MATTHEW HOLM

RANDOM HOUSE NEW YORK

AS THE NARRATOR, I REALLY FEEL THAT I SHOULD GET AT LEAST ONE LINE OF CREDIT.

Published in the United States by Random House Children's Books,
a division of Random House LLC, a Penguin Random House Company, New York.

Random House and the colophon are registered trademarks of Random House LLC.

Visit us on the Web!
randomhouse.com/kids
Babymouse.com

Educators and librarians, for a variety of teaching tools, visit us at
RHTeachersLibrarians.com

Library of Congress Cataloging-in-Publication Data
Holm, Jennifer L.
Babymouse : cupcake tycoon / by Jennifer L. Holm and Matthew Holm. — 1st ed.
p. cm.
Summary: When her school library holds a fundraiser, the imaginative Babymouse is determined to sell the most cupcakes and win the grand prize.
ISBN 978-0-375-86573-2 (trade) — ISBN 978-0-375-96573-9 (lib. bdg.)
1. Graphic novels. [1. Graphic novels. 2. Imagination—Fiction. 3. Contests—Fiction. 4. Libraries—Fiction. 5. Schools—Fiction. 6. Mice—Fiction.]
I. Holm, Matthew. II. Title. III. Title: Cupcake tycoon.
PZ7.7.H65Baf 2009 741.5'973—dc22 2009047346

MANUFACTURED IN MALAYSIA 20 19 18 17 16 15 14 13 12 11 10

Random House Children's Books supports the First Amendment
and celebrates the right to read.

SHE KNOWS HOW TO WRITE GOOD COPY!
FOR JILL APPLEBAUM

WELCOME TO THE ANCESTRAL ESTATE OF LORD BABYMOUSE . . .

"DUKE OF LOST HOMEWORK."

LORD BABYMOUSE'S GREAT-GRANDFATHER MADE THE FAMILY FORTUNE IN THE LUCRATIVE CUPCAKE TRADE.

TODAY, LORD BABYMOUSE ENJOYS THE SIMPLE PLEASURES OF A COUNTRY GENTLEMAN . . .

THANK YOU, WILSON.
WOULD YOU CARE FOR POTATO WEDGES OR TATER TOTS, LORD BABYMOUSE?

FEED YOUR BRAIN!
BLINK!

POTATO WEDGES OR TATER TOTS? YOU'RE HOLDING UP THE LINE!

UHH . . .

TATER TOTS!

MAY I PEEL YOU A TATER TOT, LORD BABYMOUSE?
YECH.

AFTER LUNCH.
HI, BABYMOUSE.
HI, WILSON.

YOU REMEMBER YOUR BOOK FOR THE LIBRARY?
IT'S HERE SOMEWHERE.

RIIIIINNNGG!
SEE YOU IN LIBRARY!

NOW WHERE IS THAT BOOK AGAIN?

WHAT'S THIS?
ANCIENT TOME

OOOH!
Really, Really Old Testament

THAT LOOKS LIKE INTERESTING READING, BABYMOUSE.
SWOOOOSH!
I'VE BEEN LOOKING FOR THAT!
GRAB!
I GUESS WE'LL NEVER KNOW.
13

LATER.
LIBRARY
EXCITED, BABYMOUSE?
THE LIBRARY IS MY FAVORITE PLACE!

THE FALL OF THE HOUSE OF US...
THE LIBRARY

BABYMOUSE?
BABYMOUSE?
BLINK!
RETURNS

COOLEST LIBRARIAN EVER!
MISS BEE!
LOVES THE DEWEY DECIMALS!
YOU CAN CHOOSE A BOOK, BABYMOUSE.

THE TOMB OF THE UNKNOWN FRACTION.
2/3 + 3/4
9/16
10/8
5/8
3/15
4/7
15/2
2/5
3/4

CREAK!

ZWECK!
ZIP!
DUCK!
ZIP!
TOIINNNGG...
PLUCK!
WHEW!

GOLD!

THE LOST CUPCAKE!

UNGH!

FINALLY!

GRARGH!

AAAAGH!

AAAAGH!

BLINK!

WHUH—OH!

WHOA!

GRAB!

CREEEEAAK...

WHEW!

THAT WAS A CLOSE CALL, BABYMOUSE.

CRACK!

FOOSH!

FWOOOSH!
I REALLY HOPE IT'S A GOOD BOOK, BABYMOUSE.
UGH. ME TOO.

THE NEXT DAY AT SCHOOL.
BECAUSE OF THE RECENT— AHEM— **DISASTER** IN THE LIBRARY . . .
I'D BE UNDER MY DESK BY NOW IF I WERE YOU, BABYMOUSE.
. . . WE ARE GOING TO HAVE A SCHOOL FUND-RAISER TO REPLACE THE BOOKS RUINED IN THE FLOOD.
GROAN.
I HATE FUND-RAISERS.
GROAN. ME TOO.

PREVIOUS FUND-RAISERS.
WANT TO BUY A MAGAZINE?

NO.

SLAM!

WANT TO BUY A CANDLE?
NO!

A TOOTHPICK HOLDER?
NO!

WANT TO BUY A POSTER?
NO!

SOME ANTI-GRAVITY BOOTS?
NO!

AN ARMADILLO?
NO!

FOR THE LAST TIME, I'M NOT FOR SALE.
NOW PUT ME DOWN!
SORRY.

WE WILL BE SELLING . . . CUPCAKES.

CUPCAKES?!!?
CUPCAKES??

A DREAM COME TRUE!

ERP.

NOW THIS IS A FUND-RAISER I CAN GET BEHIND!
ME TOO!

THE TOP FUND-RAISER WILL WIN . . .

I LOVE FRACTIONS!
A SPECIAL PRIZE!

OOOOOOUOODOOH!

WOW! I WONDER WHAT IT IS!

SCOOTER!
HELICOPTER!
FANCY VIDEO-GAME SYSTEM!
PERSONAL MOVIE THEATER!
VIRTUAL-REALITY HELMET!
SPEEDBOAT!
VROOOOM!

RIIIIIINNGGG!!!
THIS IS GOING TO BE GREAT! I JUST KNOW I'M GOING TO WIN!

BECAUSE OF YOUR TRACK RECORD OF EXCELLENT SALESMANSHIP?
GRUMBLE GRUMBLE . . .

END OF THE DAY.

RIIINGGG!!!

WHAM!

PANT
PANT
RRRRRUUUUMMMMMBBLE...

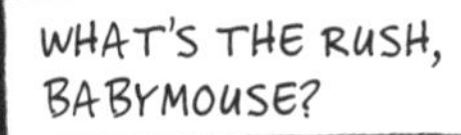
WHAT'S THE RUSH, BABYMOUSE?

HUFF! HUFF! HAVE TO—HUFF!—HURRY HOME AND—PUFF!—START SELLING BEFORE THE OTHER KIDS—PUFF!—GET TO THE NEIGHBORHOOD! PUFF!

ZIP!

THUNK!

ZIP!

SNATCH!

WOLF!
MUNCH MUNCH
SLURP!

HOW WAS SCHOOL, BABYMOUSE—?
CAN'T TALK! GOTTA SELL!
SWISH!

I'M SURE THERE'S A LESSON IN HERE FOR THE ECONOMISTS.

LATER.
TOO LATE!
OOF!

SO UNFAIR!

SLUMP

PUT ME DOWN FOR ONE CUPCAKE, BABYMOUSE.
JUST ONE?

SORRY, I ALREADY BOUGHT FROM THAT ARMADILLO.
TYPICAL.

THAT NIGHT AT DINNER.
HOW ARE THE CUPCAKE SALES GOING, BABYMOUSE?

NOT GOOD. THERE'RE TOO MANY KIDS IN THE NEIGHBORHOOD.
SHRUG
WHAT ABOUT FAMILY?

YOU WANT TO BUY SOME CUPCAKES?

I'LL BUY A FEW, BABYMOUSE. BUT WHAT I MEAN IS, WHY DON'T YOU ASK SOME RELATIVES?

THAT'S A GREAT IDEA!

YOU WANT TO BUY SOME CUPCAKES, SQUEAK?
NO, BABYMOUSE. FOR TRUCK!
BUT CUPCAKES ARE MUCH **BETTER** THAN TRUCKS, SQUEAK.
WAAAAAAAHH!!!
BABYMOUSE!

LATER.
HMM. WHO ELSE CAN I TRY?

BEEP
BOOP
BLOOP

HELLO?
HI, GRAMPAMOUSE.

IT'S BABYMOUSE!
WHO DID YOU SAY YOU WERE?

BABYMOUSE! I'M SELLING CUPCAKES!
WE DON'T HAVE A BABY IN THE HOUSE.
THIS IS AN OVER-FIFTY-FIVE COMMUNITY.

BABYMOUSE!
YOUR GRAND-DAUGHTER!
OH, BABYMOUSE. WHY DIDN'T YOU SAY SO IN THE FIRST PLACE?

GRAMPAMOUSE, I'M SELLING CUPCAKES FOR A SCHOOL FUND-RAISER. DO YOU WANT TO BUY SOME?
OF COURSE, KIDDO!
PUT ME DOWN FOR A BAKER'S DOZEN!

GREAT!
WAIT A MINUTE— THEY DON'T HAVE SUGAR IN THEM, DO THEY? I'M NOT ALLOWED TO EAT SUGAR.

WELL, AT LEAST HE HAS A GOOD EXCUSE, BABYMOUSE.
EVERYONE HAS A GOOD EXCUSE.
TYPICAL.

THE NEXT MORNING.
BUS STOP
I'VE SOLD A HUNDRED CUPCAKES SO FAR. I KNOW I'M GOING TO BE THE TOP SELLER.
WOW!
THAT'S GREAT, FELICIA!
ONE HUNDRED? I'VE GOT TO FIGURE OUT HOW TO SELL MORE!
ESPECIALLY SINCE YOUR MOM AND I ARE THE ONLY ONES WHO HAVE BOUGHT ANY SO FAR.

LATER AT SCHOOL.
I WANT YOU TO GRASP THE ROPE AND CLIMB AS HIGH AS YOU CAN.
ALL RIGHT, LET'S SEE. WE'VE GOT FELICIA AND BABYMOUSE UP FIRST.
RUMPELSTILTSKIN
MOVE IT, BABYMOUSE!
EEP!

READY . . .
GO!

I NEED TO SPIN THIS STRAW INTO GOLD!
GOOD LUCK WITH THAT. YOU CAN'T EVEN SELL CUPCAKES.
HEY! GET OUT OF MY FAIRY TALE!
POOF!
NEED SOME HELP?
YOU KNOW HOW TO SPIN STRAW INTO GOLD?

WELL, I READ ABOUT IT ON THE INTERNET.
WHIRRRRRRR
SPINNNN
CREAK CREAK
WOW!
GOLD!
HAND ME SOME MORE STRAW!
SURE THING!

WHIRRRRR
CREAK
CREAK

WHIRRR

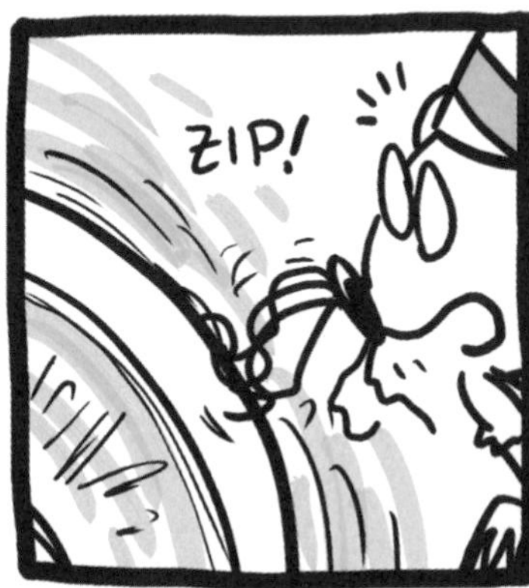
ZIP!

AAAH!
YOINK!
SWOOP!

WHIIIIZZZZZZZZZZZZZZ

I LIKE THE SHORTER WHISKERS, BABYMOUSE. VERY STYLISH.
SNIP!
TYPICAL.

LATER AT SCHOOL.
CUPCAKES
GOOD TO THE LAST CRUMB!
~Felicia

THAT'S A GOOD SLOGAN.

AFTER SCHOOL.
WHAT ARE YOU DOING, BABYMOUSE?
I'M MAKING ADVERTISING POSTERS.
HOW ENTERPRISING.

THERE!
YUMMY CUPCAKES!
BUY SOME!
-BABYMOUSE-
555-3709

HONK!

Cupcakes by Felicia

JAW.
THUNK!

SHE DEFINITELY HAS A CAREER IN ADVERTISING AHEAD OF HER.
VROOM!
SIGH.

THE NEXT MORNING.
MY RADIO CAMPAIGN STARTS TODAY, AND THEN THE ONLINE ADS WILL ROLL OUT TOMORROW!
WOW! YOU'LL WIN THE BIG PRIZE FOR SURE!
COMIX
GREEK MYTHS (THEY HAPPENED A LONG TIME AGO)
THE STORY OF KING MIDAS
EVERYTHING HE TOUCHED TURNED TO GOLD!

ANCIENT GREECE.
KING BABYMIDAS, I GRANT YOU ONE WISH.
DIONYSUS
A GOD!

I WANT THE POWER TO TURN WHATEVER I TOUCH INTO CUPCAKES!

ZAP!

TAP

PROINK!

PROINK!

THAT POOR ARMADILLO.

UH-OH.
EVIL IDEA BREWING
EGYPT.
POIT!
ALL RIGHT!

BABYMOUSE, THE MORAL OF THE STORY IS THAT HAVING A GOLDEN TOUCH ISN'T GOOD. IT'S GREEDY.
HEY! THIS IS MY MYTH! TAKE YOUR MORAL SOMEPLACE ELSE!

?
RRRRRUUUMMMBLE

RRRRUMMBLE...

YIPE!

WHUMP!

BLINK!

BUMP!

WHUMP!

HOW MANY CUPCAKES HAVE **YOU** SOLD, BABYMOUSE?

UH, TWO. I MEAN, THREE!

BOY, YOU'VE SURE GOT THE **MIDAS TOUCH.**

SEE, WOULDN'T THE MORAL HAVE BEEN LESS EMBARRASSING IN YOUR PRIVATE DAYDREAM RATHER THAN OUT HERE IN THE REAL WORLD?

HA! HA! HA!
HA! HA! HA!
SIGH.

LUNCH.

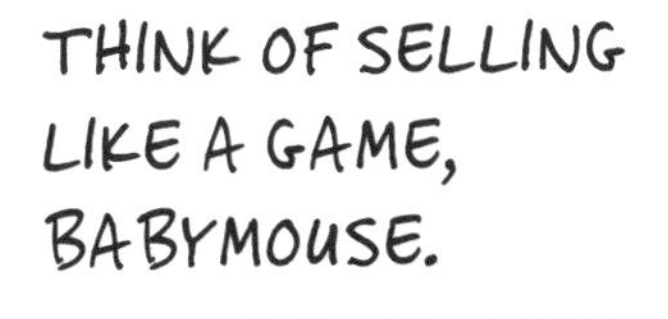
THINK OF SELLING LIKE A GAME, BABYMOUSE.

CUPCAKE SALES!
MOM 2
NARRATOR 1
HMMM...

HOMEWORK
NEIGHBOR'S SCARY DOG BITES!
ANNOYING NARRATOR BERATES YOU AGAIN!
TSK-TSK.
-2
DODGEBALL!
OW!
SELL THREE TO A RELATIVE!
$
$
$
MEAN GIRL
HISS!

ZZZ
SLEEP.
MOM TAKES PITY ON YOU.
BUYS FOUR!
RECESS
BONUS!
BONUS!
CUPCAKE TYCOON
— THE GAME —
LOCKER!
RAID PIGGY BANK!
SECRET PRIZE

CLACK!
GET OUT OF HOMEWORK! FOREVER!!!
I WON!
I WON!
UH, BABYMOUSE. YOU'RE NOT EVEN PLAYING.
STUPID BOARD GAME.

AFTER SCHOOL.
U-NEEDIT!
NOW!
I'M HERE TO TELL YOU ABOUT THE "U-NEEDIT"!
IT DOES EVERYTHING!
SLICES! DICES! RINSES! MINCES!
WRITES THANK-YOU NOTES!
FOLDS LAUNDRY!
EMPTIES THE LITTER BOX!
OPERATORS ARE STANDING BY!!!
OVER 40 MILLION "U-NEEDITS" HAVE BEEN SOLD ON TV!
CALL 1-800-YOU-~~WANT~~ NEED-IT!
40 MILLION?
$$
CHA-CHING!

WHAT ARE YOU UP TO NOW, BABYMOUSE?

I'M GOING TO SHOOT A TV COMMERCIAL!

ACTION!

UH . . .

UM . . .

UH . . .
THIS IS WHY YOU PAY FOR TALENT.

MUCH LATER.
BUY CUPCAKES!
1-555-5309

DO YOU THINK IT'S A GOOD IDEA TO PUT YOUR PHONE NUMBER ON THAT, BABYMOUSE?

SURE!

I'M JUST GOING TO PUT IT ON THE WEB!

WWW.YOUSEELOTSOFSILLYVIDEOS.COM

CLICK!

ONE SECOND LATER.
RING!

TWO SECONDS LATER.
RING! RING!

BABYMOUSE!! DID YOU GIVE OUT OUR PHONE NUMBER?!?!

RING!
EEP.
RING!
RING!
RING!
MAYBE THAT'S HOLLYWOOD CALLING, BABYMOUSE.

THAT NIGHT.
BABYMOUSE, ONE OF MY COWORKERS BOUGHT TWO CUPCAKES.
GREAT, DAD. THAT MAKES FIVE.
WHAT'S WRONG, BABYMOUSE?
I'LL NEVER BE ABLE TO SELL AS MANY AS FELICIA! SHE'S SO MUCH BETTER AT THIS THAN ME!
THUNK!
NOT TO MENTION, SHE HAS THAT ADVERTISING AGENCY WORKING FOR HER.
YEAH, THAT TOO.

WELL, BABYMOUSE, JUST REMEMBER THE REAL REASON YOU'RE SELLING CUPCAKES.

THE GRAND PRIZE!
???
???

THE **LIBRARY**, REMEMBER? WHAT AM I GOING TO DO WITH YOU?

I REALLY HOPE IT'S A HELICOPTER!

THAT NIGHT.
WHIRRRRRRRRRRRRR.

BM

WHIRRRRRR

WHUP
WHUP WHUP

MR. BABYMOUSE? I'M DOING A PROFILE OF YOU FOR **MOUSE MONEY** MAGAZINE.

YOU'RE THE MOST SUCCESSFUL BUSINESSMAN IN THE WORLD. CAN YOU TELL ME HOW YOU BUILT YOUR EMPIRE?

WITH A LOT OF HARD WORK AND . . .
SCRIBBLE

. . . A CORNER CUPCAKE STAND.

A CORNER CUPCAKE STAND!

OPERATION: CUPCAKE STAND

1. CHOOSE LOCATION!

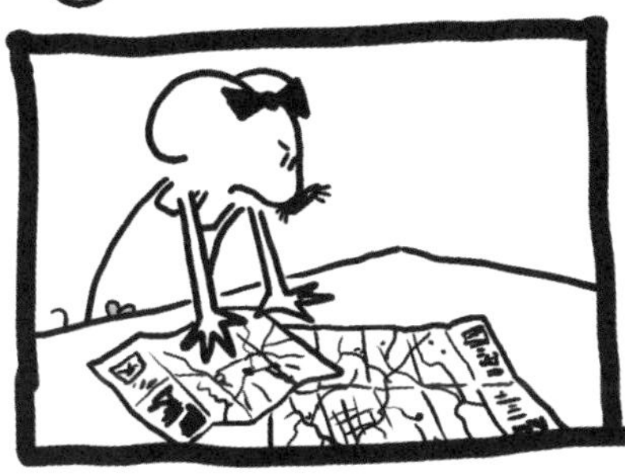

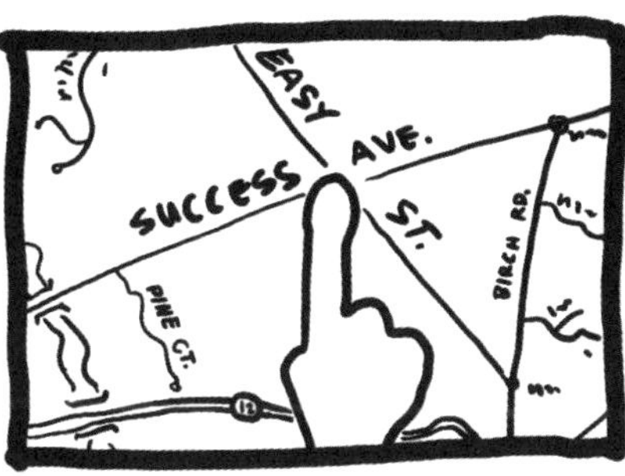

2. WRITE CLEVER SLOGAN!

3. BUILD STOREFRONT!

CATCHY SLOGAN, BABYMOUSE.
EASY ST.
SUCCESS AVE.
SPORTING GOODS
BABYMOUSE'S BAKE SALE
THANKS!
ONE CUPCAKE = ONE BOOK!

WHIRRRRR...
WHIRRRRRRRRRRRRR...
FELICIA'S CUPCAKES: ALMOST AS SWEET AS ME!
THAT SURE IS SOME COPYWRITER SHE'S GOT.
TYPICAL.

LATER.
BABYMOUSE'S BAKE SALE
ONE CUPCAKE = ONE BOOK!
ONE CUPCAKE = ONE BOOK!

THAT'S A GREAT CAUSE! PUT ME DOWN FOR THREE CUPCAKES.

YOUR FIRST **REAL** CUSTOMER, BABYMOUSE!

HOW SWEET! CUPCAKES FOR BOOKS!
BABYMOUSE'S BAKE SALE
WHAT A DARLING FUND-RAISER! GIVE ME FIVE CUPCAKES!
CUPCAKE
NE BOOK!

CRACK!

UH-OH.

BABYMOUSE'S BAKE SALE
ONE CUPCAKE = ONE BOOK!
ZWIP!
ZWIP!
ZWIP!

THUNK!
THUNK!
OW!
OW!
HAIL!

AAAGH!
MEOW!
WOOF!
CATS & DOGS!

ARMADILLOS!
NOT AGAIN!
HEY!
BONK!

THIS IS LIKE A GREEK TRAGEDY.

MEANWHILE . . .
NEWS 5
SPLOOSH!

SLOW NEWS DAY. WE REALLY NEED A STORY.

?

BAKE SALE
ONE CUPCAKE
ONE BOOK

THAT'S THE SADDEST THING I'VE EVER SEEN! STOP THE VAN!

SCREECH!

HI, I'M MARGARET MAGPIE, CHANNEL 5 NEWS.
BABYMOUSE'S
KE SALE
CAN I ASK WHAT YOU'RE DOING?
I'M TRYING TO SELL CUPCAKES. IT'S FOR OUR SCHOOL FUND-RAISER TO BUY LIBRARY BOOKS.
KE SALE
ONE CUPCAKE
THAT'S SOME KIND OF DEDICATION, TO KEEP SELLING DESPITE THIS WEATHER! YOU MUST REALLY LOVE BOOKS.

I....
I....
BIG PRIZE

GLAMOUR!
EXCITEMENT!
ADVENTURE!
CRUNCH!
CRACK!
RRRRRUUMMMMBBLE...

I DO.
I LOVE BOOKS.

I LOVE BOOKS.

I LOVE BOOKS.

I LOVE BOOKS.

I LOVE BOOKS.
私は本が大好きです

CUP
CAKES
PATHETIC MOUSE SELLS CUP
I LOVE BOOKS.
TIMES SQ
305

?
I'LL TAKE THREE!

A FEW DAYS LATER.
READ! (duh.)
YOU SOLD TWENTY THOUSAND CUPCAKES, BABYMOUSE. VERY IMPRESSIVE.

IMPRESSIVE INDEED. AND HAVE YOU FIGURED OUT HOW YOU'RE GOING TO DELIVER THEM TO JAPAN?

I'M GOING TO BORROW WILSON'S SKATEBOARD!

OPENING DAY FOR THE NEW LIBRARY.
LOOKS LIKE ALL YOUR HARD WORK WAS WORTH IT, HUH, BABYMOUSE?
WOW!

OPENING-DAY CEREMONY.

AND FOR SELLING THE MOST CUPCAKES, WE WOULD LIKE TO HONOR **BABYMOUSE** WITH THE **GRAND PRIZE.**

SWISH!
A PLAQUE?

IT'S ENGRAVED WITH YOUR NAME.
WITH GREAT APPRECIATION TO BABYMOUSSE

ACTUALLY, I KIND OF LIKE "BABYMOUSSE."

TYPICAL.

WITH GREAT
APPRECIATION
TO
BABYMOUSSE

FOR PERFECT
WHISKERS
EVERY TIME!

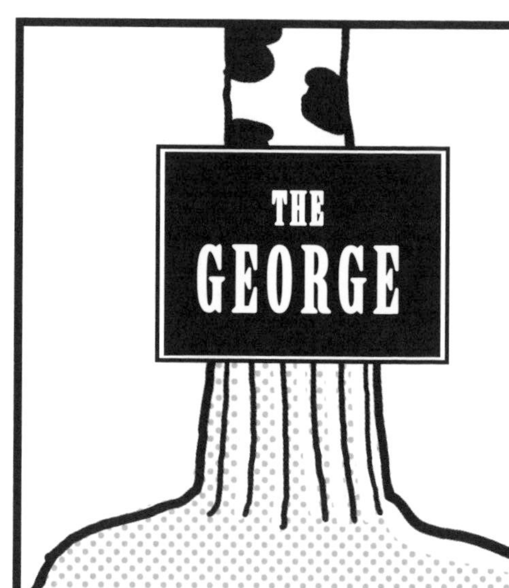

SQUEAK'S
BOO-BOO CREAM
SNIFF.
To take the sting away

WILSON'S
Frozen Waffles
A healthy breakfast on the bus!

The Sweet Smell of Success!
Felicia
PARFUM

BIG PINK ERASER
TEACHERS EVERYWHERE AGREE:
IT'S BEST FOR HOMEWORK!

THE SUPER WORLD OF MARIO

Wii
Wii
HOME
A
1
2
3+
TM

Wii
SUPER MARIO GALAXY
MARIO
3
www.pegi.info
PAL
Nintendo

This book is available in quantity at special discounts for your group or organization.
For further information, contact:

Triumph Books LLC
814 North Franklin Street
Chicago, Illinois 60610
Phone: (312) 337-0747
www.triumphbooks.com

Printed in U.S.A.
ISBN: 978-1-62937-589-2

Content packaged by Mojo Media, Inc.
Joe Funk: Editor
Jason Hinman: Creative Director

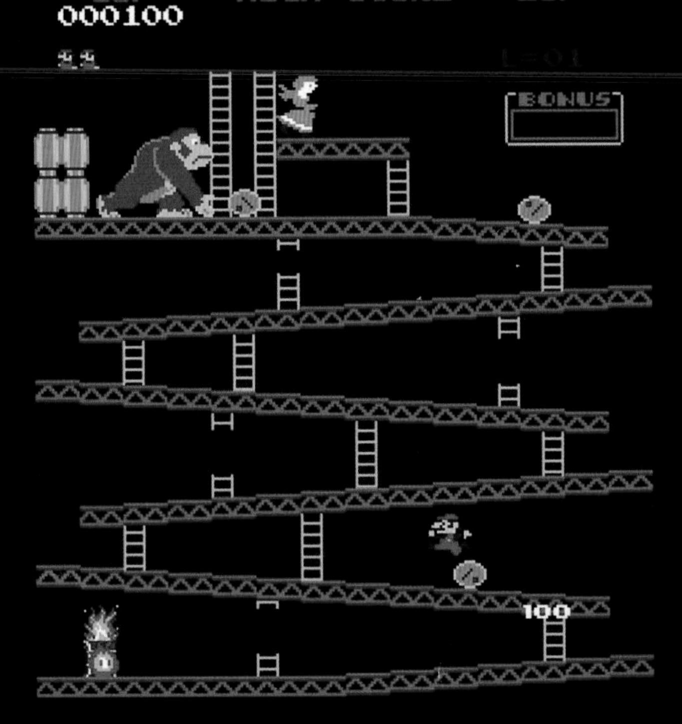

CONTENTS

INTRODUCTION 6
THE BEGINNING 10
THE 1980s 16
THE 1990s 24
THE 2000s 34
THE 2010s 40
SUPER MARIO ODYSSEY STRATEGY 44

INTRODUCTION

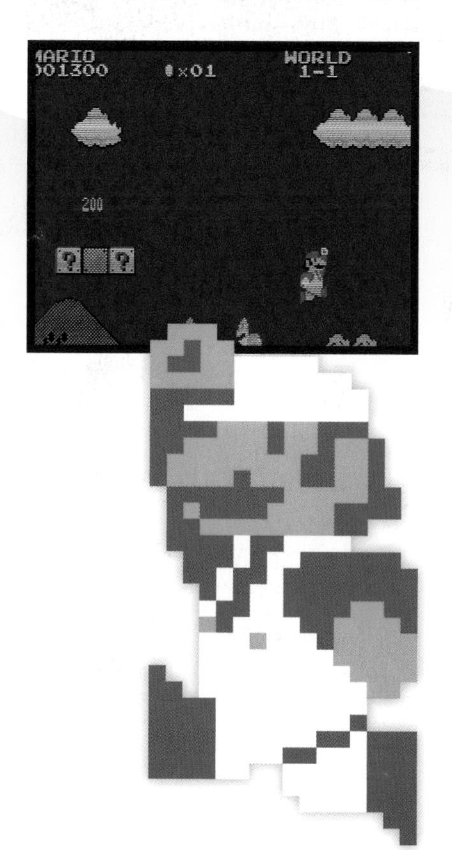

Mario has been around for years, starting out in the early 80's, everyone thought that this little character had real promise. The creators had him in a different game originally, but soon gave him his own game because everyone loved the little guy.

Mario is now one of the biggest characters of all time, but the game makers with Nintendo didn't know that when they put him in Donkey Kong. They just felt that this little tradesman had a role to play in the world taken over by the massive gorilla.

Having appeared in over 200 video games since he was created, he has gained a lot of fame throughout the Nintendo world and still continues to have not only games of his own, but also movies, shows and much more that feature him and his brother Luigi.

One of the biggest and best selling franchises of all time, Mario has gone to the top of the charts with many of his games and even some he's featured in as well. Super Mario set the scene for him, but then came his other signature games such as Mario Kart, Mario's Time Machine, Mario Tennis and so many more.

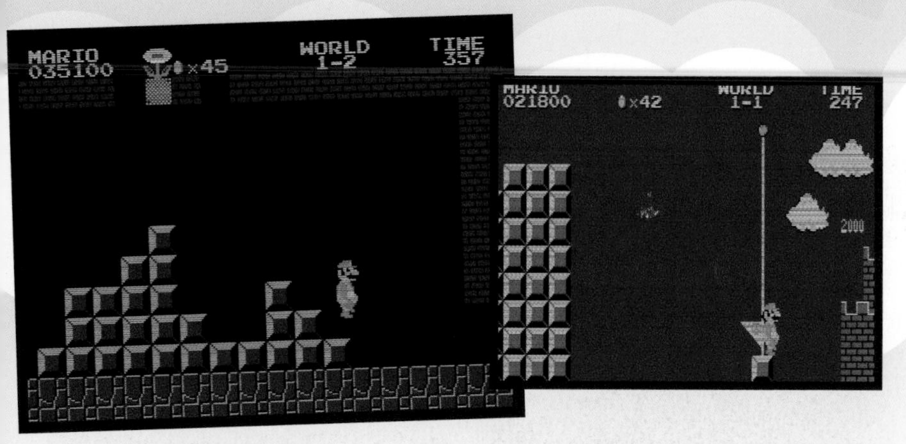

With all the games out there, Mario continues to be a loved character for so many. Players looking for quality games with a character they know well instinctively turn toward Mario titles, and he continues to be a favorite for many.

NINTENDO'S BEGINNINGS

Nintendo wasn't always just a video and game console maker for players. The company started small as a trading card platform, helping players trade and play, and as a toy maker. They didn't dive into the game console business until many of the consoles became bigger and more well known.

With this new technology, the group that was working inside a tiny office space then developed not only a new game but a new system. This led to the evolution of Nintendo itself. It was something that would make them much bigger than Pac Man, as well as any of the other game makers out there.

To this day Nintendo continues to top the charts with their games and game consoles, many of which are currently handheld, making a big impact on the way that gaming is done today.

They're the gaming systems you know and use currently.

MARIO'S CREATION

Mario had a humble beginning as a side-story character for the hit game Donkey Kong. The makers had no idea Mario would go as far as he did. Donkey Kong was one of the first ambitious game projects by Nintendo that the creators hoped would become as big as Pac Man.

While Donkey Kong did make it quite big, he wasn't able to beat out that mega-successful dot eating character.

As the creators realized how popular Mario was, they decided to give him a name, give him a background and then present him in a new game, a game all his own, that people could really enjoy.

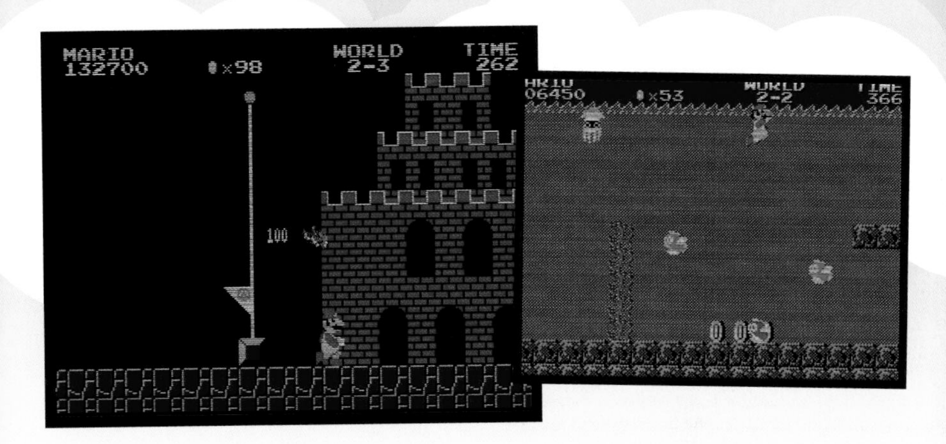

Naming the character also gave a face and a purpose to the little pixelated guy. After a bit of a debate the creators settled on Mario as his name, but head creator Shigeru Miyamoto almost went with Mr. Video instead. If the makers had given him a name like Mr. Video, he wouldn't have made it very far. He was supposed to be personable and someone that would provide hours of fun much like a friend. A name like Mr. Video just doesn't match his theme which is why it's fortunate for Nintendo that they ended up going with Mario as the name, because they've enjoyed great success from the little jumping guy.

Over time Mario has grown and evolved. He has become better-looking due to the evolution of game systems and the way the characters and items on the screen look.

Learn more about the history of Mario and how he became as big as he is today. It won't come as a shock to know that he has a much deeper history than most people realize.

You might not have even realized that Mario has been around as long as he has, or that he's evolved so much. Your parents might have even played the original Mario games when they were younger, so ask them about how he was then, as compared to how he is now.

SUPER MARIO BROS. TAKE THE STAGE

Of course, you're very familiar with Mario, but what about his brother, Luigi? He didn't make his big entrance until some time later to provide a little more character diversification.

With Mario Bros. coming out big and in full force, many people thought that Mario's full name was Mario Bros. Nintendo finally revealed to the audience that Mario's name is actually Mario Mario, and that the "Brothers" was just the name of the game that also included Luigi in it.

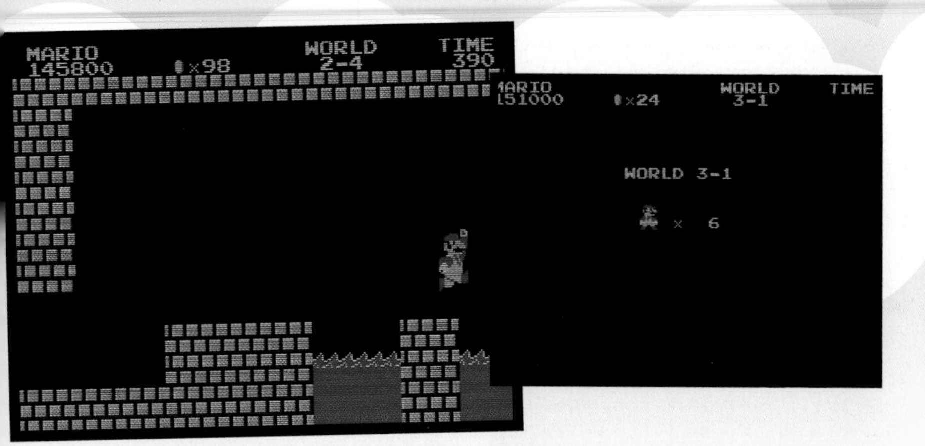

Of course, Luigi is now featured in almost every game that comes out with Mario, but he never was in the beginning. He didn't come out until 1983, a few years after Mario had already been created and introduced to the world.

When you think of Super Mario Bros. games as they are today, you're allowed to choose which character you'd like to play throughout the game, whether it is Mario, Luigi, Princess Toadstool or any of the others. That wasn't always the case though.

It's a bit shocking to find out you once were stuck just playing Mario. Read on to learn how the game's have evolved over the years and become richer with features.

What's your favorite thing about Mario? Do you have a favorite game that he is featured in? Have you played the newest Mario game that's recently been released for Nintendo Switch?

Now's the time to learn all about Mario and what the little lovable character has to offer, from the beginning of his creation onward. He's been in countless games that we know and love, and is one of the biggest video game icons today.

THE BEGINNING

Mario didn't always have the spotlight in his own games. He started off in a much humbler way than many characters do. While most new characters are given their own games in the beginning, Mario was just a side character that had to grow into the fully-fledged feature character that he is today.

Mario had to win our hearts over time, and that's probably part of the reason that he's such a well-developed character today.

He started out in the early '80s as a side character in the game Donkey Kong.

As an Italian plumber, no one thought he would go very far in the world of video games. However, with some time, he has become one of the most recognizable characters throughout the world. He is featured in over 100 video games and it's hard to imagine a world without Mario in it.

However, many people want to know where he came from? What is Mario's story?

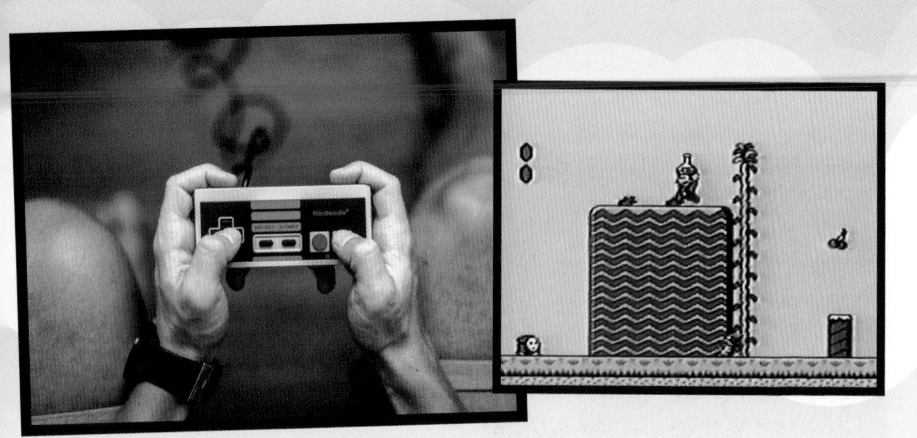

The struggling toy and card shop known as Nintendo wanted to enter the world of video games. Somewhat new to the market, these games seemed to make an impact on the world. They wanted to get into the action by creating a character that would make a difference.

They started off in the world of video games working on arcade game creations. These pixelated games meant for the public weren't as involved or developed as the games we all know today.

They tried out a few early games but to no avail, nothing stuck with the audiences that they were trying to reach. Radar Scope, one of their first games, barely sold at all. This left the company with a difficult challenge to overcome, they had to find a game that would make an impact in the gaming world. A game that would make Nintendo into a recognizable brand to gamers.

To help kickstart this dream, the company approached artist Shigeru Miyamoto. They asked him to design a game for the company, hoping that his skills with game creation would lead to a game that would sell out and hopefully bring in something for the small company.

Not a programmer, Miyamoto had to think out a story line before even being able to put together graphics that would fit into a playable game. That's something that didn't happen at the time. Creators would throw together games and work on the story line and extras as they go as more of an afterthought than anything else. As you can guess, Miyamoto's early games were a smash success. He started off with Donkey Kong, but he built a bunch of other successes as well.

Miyamoto went on to create some of the well known games of your childhood, such as Legend of Zelda, Pikmin, Star Fox, and even the Wii Sports bundle that comes with the console. He continues to work for Nintendo and is a big name within the industry.

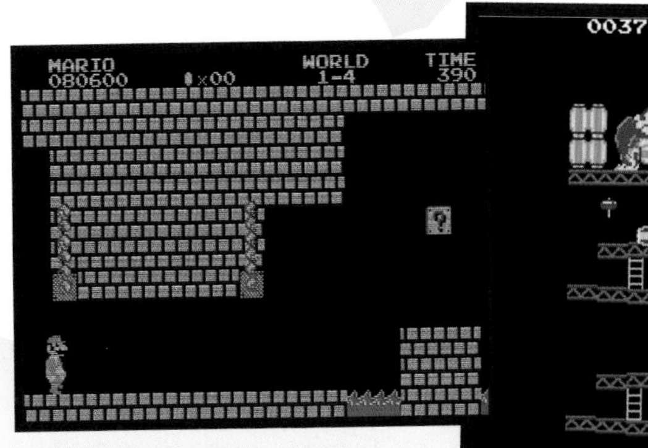

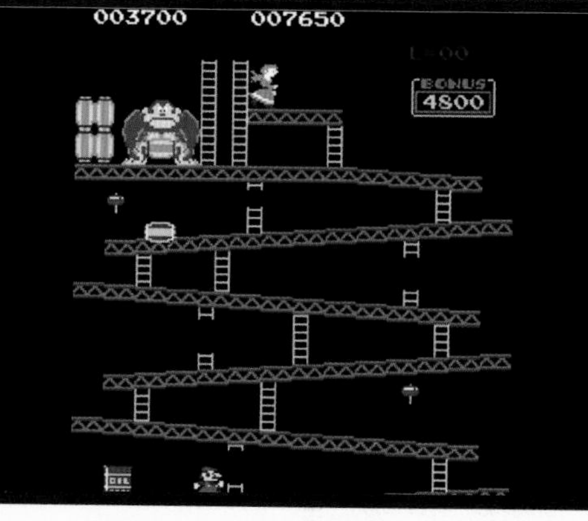

THE BIRTH OF DONKEY KONG

Hiring Miyamoto led to the creation of the game Donkey Kong. This was a game between a gorilla, a girlfriend, and a man. It was not only something that many of the producers didn't think would go far, but it was far from the video games that we know now.

Even though Mario at that time was known as "Jump Man," he still made headlines in the game. Many people wanted to see more of him. Back then, the character was only able to jump up and down, go side to side and climb ladders. With the evolution of gaming systems in the future, that quickly changed though.

Donkey Kong quickly became a fast seller in the gaming industry and all because the game makers decided to move forward with a different type of game. They created something that made headlines because the characters were more developed and had a story line.

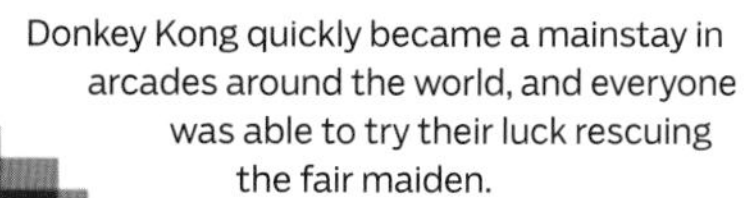

Donkey Kong quickly became a mainstay in arcades around the world, and everyone was able to try their luck rescuing the fair maiden.

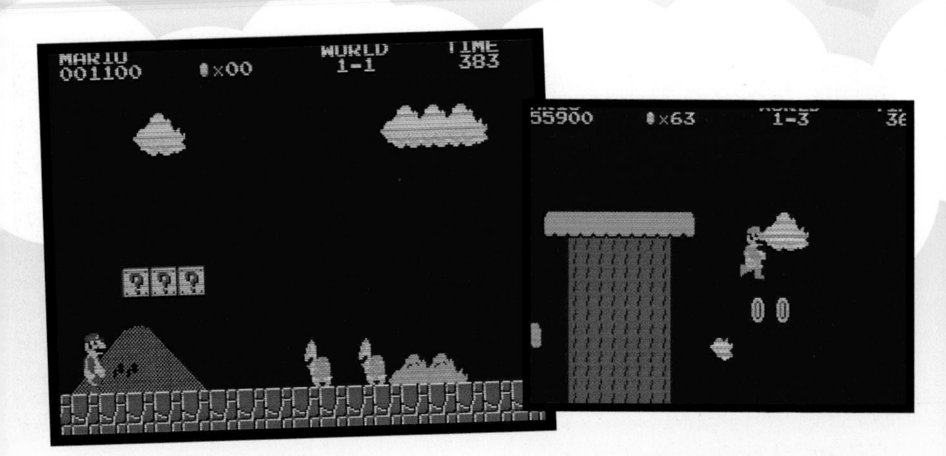

WHERE MARIO GOT HIS NAME

Everyone always asks where Mario's name came from. It's a seemingly random name, but it's one that definitely has a backstory to it and it's something that is pretty interesting.

When the team had to come up with a new game after Donkey Kong made it big, they wanted to feature little Jump Man in the game. However, with a name like Jump Man, it just wasn't going to make the impact that they wanted.

While brainstorming in their small office, they were thinking of game ideas and names for this little guy. The office owner then came in and demanded that he get rent money for the office space that they were using.

Working on getting a game out there and distributed, the landlord made a big scene while demanding the late rent money. His name? Mario. The staff members then started joking and calling the little Jump Man Mario. He looked somewhat the same, had the same overalls and the same appearance, so to this day, that's how Mario is known.

As for the landlord, he'd rather no one knew that the little character was actually named after him.

Additionally, they wanted the character to be seen as a hard worker within the industry. He needed to do a trade job that he was dedicated too. This led the developers to create him as a plumber, instead of just a general handyman that was once shown in the Donkey Kong arcade game.

This put not only a name to the character, but also a backstory for him, as well. It's something that wasn't normally done in the past but the creators felt it was necessary in order to make a connection with the players.

MOVING ON TO DIFFERENT GAMES

Since Mario was developed, the makers wanted to make a game of his own. They wanted to show the world that he was here and ready to stay for more play. With so many ideas going through the team, they had to come up with something that was not like any of the other games out there, including Donkey Kong.

He was a 'go-to' character, which put him in any spot needed, which was ideal for many different types of games that they could create focused around Mario.

The first game that featured Mario as the lead was Mario Bros. a game where Luigi was also introduced into the storyline. However, before Mario Bros. came out, Donkey Kong Junior let the world know that little Jump Man was actually named Mario before he had a chance to get his own game.

This brought a lot of attention to the Mario Bros. game that would soon hit the shelves and then sell out fairly quickly.

Read through the following chapters to learn more about the Mario games that would soon follow throughout the years. Jump Man started it all for Nintendo in Donkey Kong, but soon made a wave in the gaming world with many other appearances and all the games that he was placed in.

He was even featured in movies over the years. Find out where the Mario you know now came from and read more about his past and development by Nintendo creators, themselves.

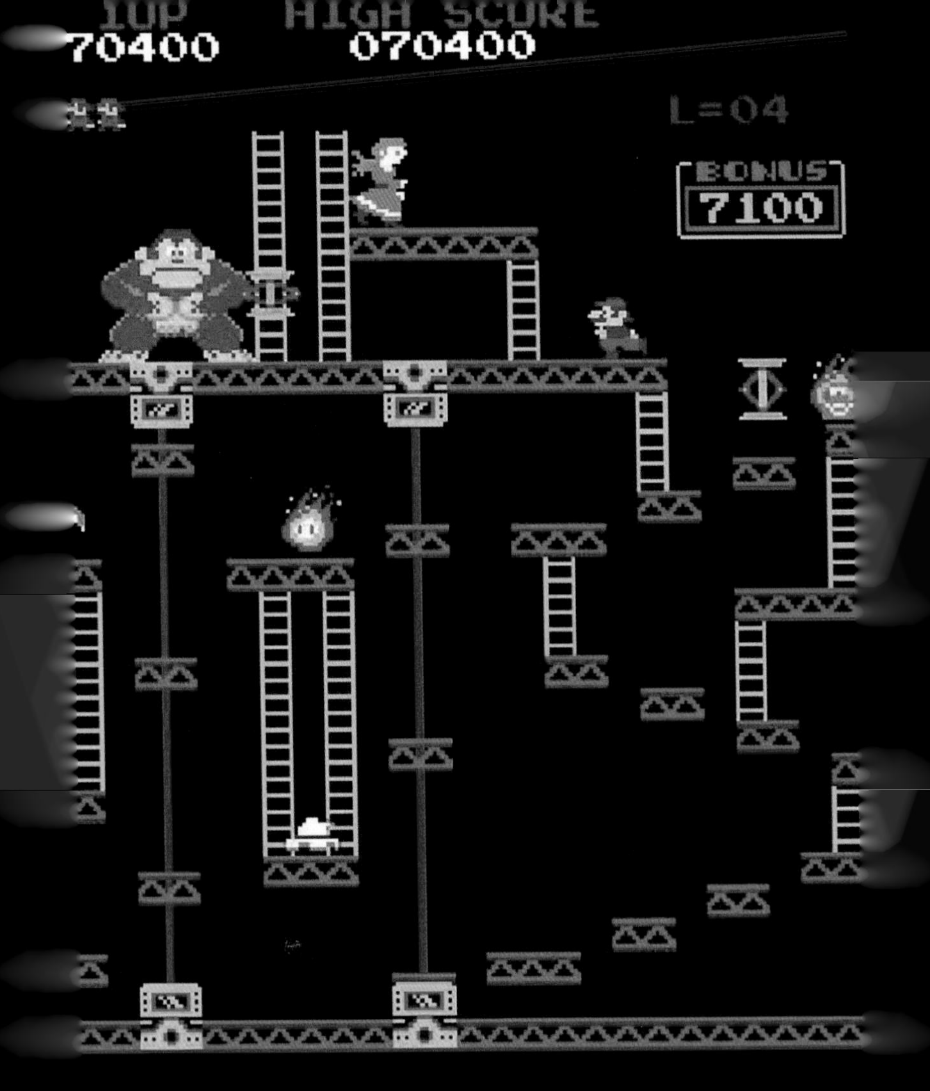
1UP
70400
HIGH SCORE
070400
L=04
BONUS
7100

MARIO OF THE 1980s

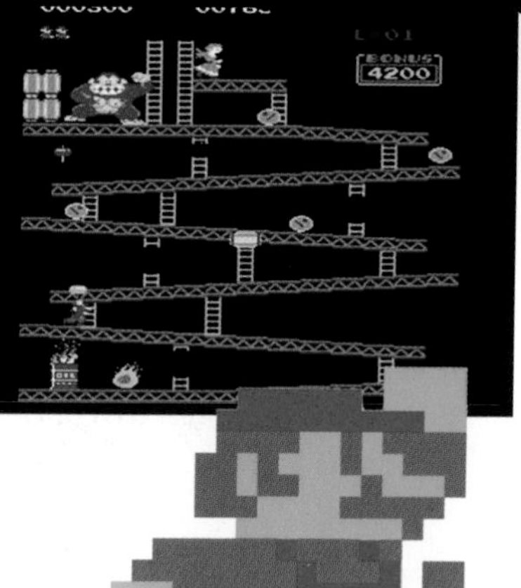

Mario started his early years known as 'Jump Man.' After a nice little makeover, he then was given the name Mario. This change gave him more graphical development and also made him into a more complex character. It allowed him to be seen throughout an ever-expanding and growing world of games.

The little guy was a big hit in the Donkey Kong games, which led developers to believe he would be ideal for a standalone set of games. This was an idea much of the rest of the world didn't agree with, they were proven wrong in a big way though. They quickly found out that Mario's debut would be a giant hit.

Mario started off big and only got bigger over the years. He continues to come out in new games ever few years and has been featured on different game systems throughout the history of Nintendo. Read on for more in-depth information about Mario's past and what made him into the rich and well-known hit character he is today.

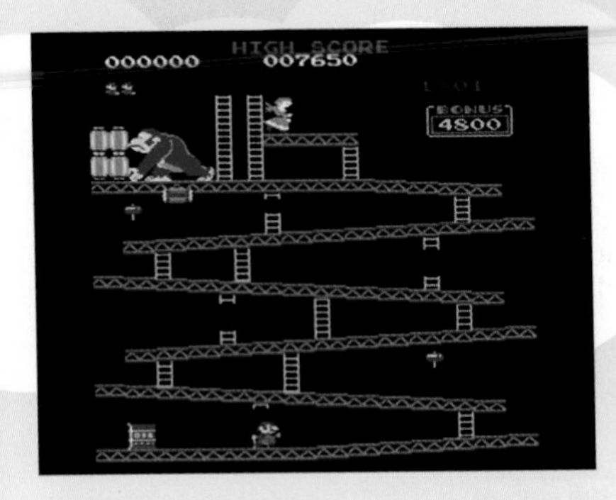

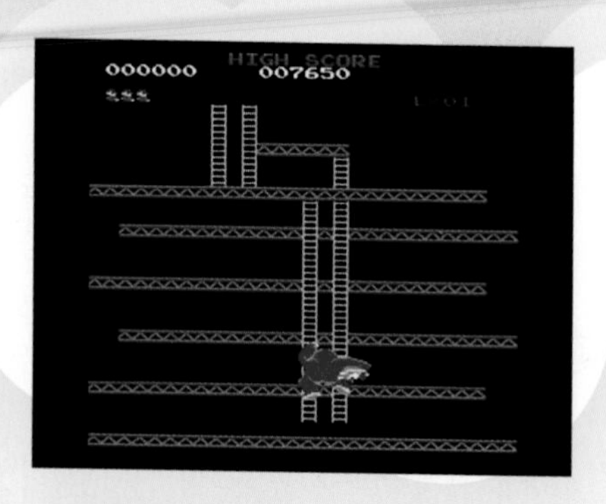

PIXELATED AND NOT WELL KNOWN

Starting out as just a pixelated character, Jump Man was featured in the Donkey Kong games. He was only able to move in small directions and climb ladders. This was something that needed improvement, but since he wasn't the star of the game, they didn't focus all of their attention on just Jump Man. Donkey Kong was the real star of the show that the creators felt that they needed to focus on.

However, after seeing how he was adored, Donkey Kong creators knew that Jump Man could have a real future, but in his own game world developed around him.

It didn't take long after this realization for Mario to become a hit success. Creators of the game put out the original, and quickly launched a whole succession of sequels building on Mario's success.

CHANGING HIS SPRITE

Enhancements were made on Mario's sprite to make him stand out on the new NES system. This was developed in 1981. This made Mario have a better look, a clear focus in the game and provide the player with better graphics overall. The NES system was designed to revolutionize gaming for players and create a graphically superior experience.

With every game thereafter, Mario kept changing his look. He'd become more focused as a person and less pixelated. His outfits would stand out more and he would have more detail.

Almost every Mario that came out would soon become something clearer and different. This was the wave of a new gaming era for those that would soon be playing on the new Nintendo systems with Mario at their side.

DID YOU KNOW?

Mario was once just a square pixelated box and they were unable to create hair that did not look funny, which is why Mario is wearing a hat in every game that he is shown in? Especially the games from the past.

Mario's look has changed so often that sometimes the early Mario characters are known as Mario's dark times. This is because the little guy on the original games looks nothing like the full-fledged character that we're all so familiar with today.

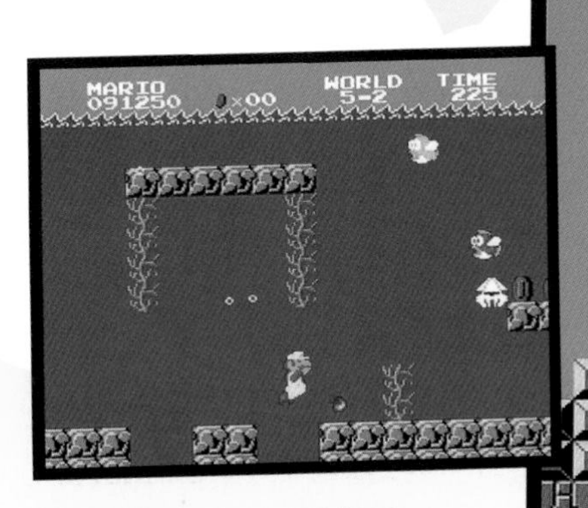

THE CONSOLES OF THE '80S

The Nintendo Entertainment System (NES) was the first-ever home gaming system that would feature Mario and his friends. This system was much different from the arcade games where the games would have to be played and were normally in public areas not in homes of the players. This system was released in 1983, allowing for those that loved Mario to bring the action from the arcade to their home.

The Nintendo Game Boy was the next device to come out and provide users with a way to play Mario on the go. Sure it was large, and ate batteries with a huge appetite, but the cool new device allowed players to bring the fun with them on black and white screens with pixelated characters everywhere. The Game Boy came out in 1989 and the makers of Mario would have to find ways to create a game that would transfer from the NES to the Game Boy system without an issue.

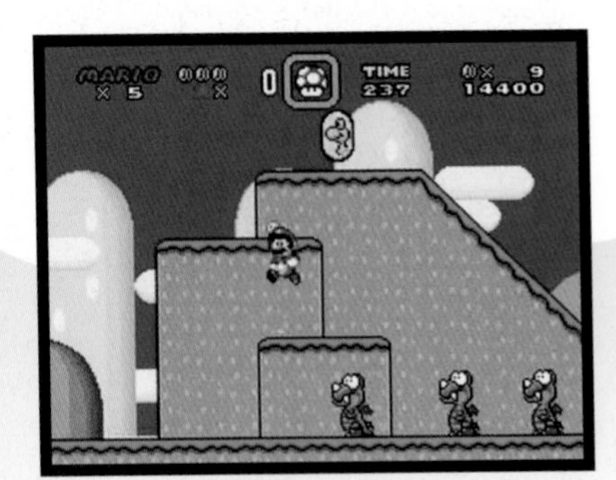

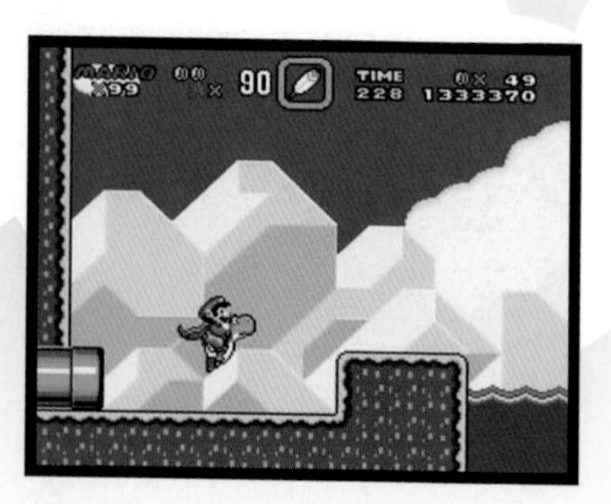

WE WELCOME MARIO BROS

Times changed for Mario after his initial release and in 1983, Mario Bros was established. This was an arcade-style game where you could play on your own or 1v1 against your brother Luigi. Of course, while playing alone, you had to go through the two tier, 2 pipe, turtle and mushroom infested level all on your own. This was a challenge that many gamers accepted.

A lot of players from this time would fixate on the game, because it was revolutionary for its time. There were many obstacles and challenges other games simply didn't have back then. The uniqueness of Mario Bros was mostly due to the creators with Nintendo creating a story line, instead of throwing items together and calling it a game like many other creators during that time period.

This was the first game where Mario is known to be a plumber, and also the game that welcomes his brother Luigi to the game. It was also the first game where Mario was the main character and not Jump Man that was featured in a Donkey Kong game, though he was Mario in Donkey Kong Junior that had released a year earlier.

SUPER MARIO BROS. FOLLOWS

Two years later, every player was excited to see a new game evolve with Mario, Super Mario Bros. This was the first game where Mario had to rescue a princess in distress. Bowser was also featured in this version of Mario. Many new characters, faces, items and obstacles were then presented. Not only that, but Mario ended up going through quite the make over to get here. This was to keep up with the new graphics of the gaming system, which made a huge difference on the way that Mario was presented throughout the game.

Super Mario Bros. 2 was released shortly after the first. The first had done so well, the makers wanted to release another. The second version was released in 1988, followed by a third version. Super Mario Bros. 3 sold out more copies than other console games throughout the entire world. This was in 1989, when the game makers were slowing production of games, but would soon come up with another Mario game to send out to the world.

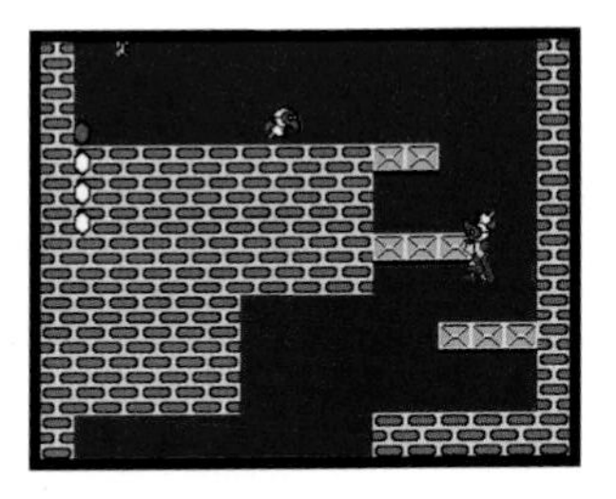

DID YOU KNOW?

Super Mario Bros. 2 was not originally a Super Mario Bros. game. It was known as Doki Doki Panic. Replacing the original characters of the game with Super Mario Bros. characters, it became a Mario game.

This is the only Mario game to feature Wart as a main boss. It also gives players the opportunity to be other Mario characters, not just Mario or Luigi.

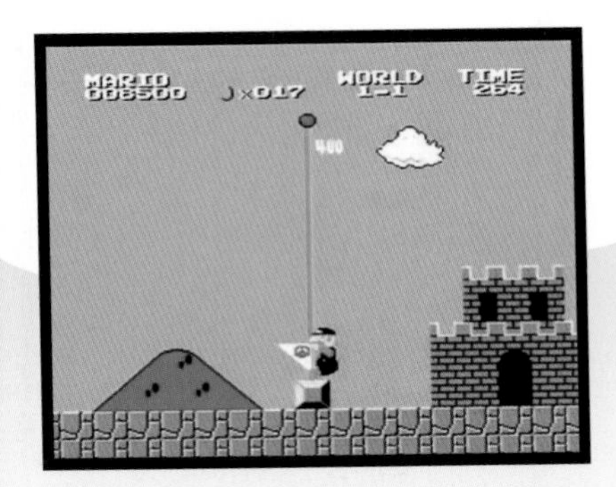

In both of these games, the player's main goal is to help Mario track down the princess, defeat the bosses and in the later versions they can even play as any of the Mario characters that they would like to be. These games brought more variation to the table, allowing the players to have a bit more control.

With even more features to the game, this quickly became a popular choice for many people out there searching for a game that would deliver. All three versions of Super Mario, were able to do just that and keep someone occupied for hours.

Even today the original Super Mario Bros. games are ported to the latest Nintendo game consoles. They've been redone again and again and still remain one of the most beloved of all the Nintendo games ever released. Mario is one of the most original Nintendo games and will remain as one of the favorites even if Nintendo stops releasing the games.

SUPER MARIO LAND TOWARDS THE END

Nearing the end of the '80s, Super Mario Land was the one that bid the '80s goodbye. The game features a more detailed sprite to play with. This gave a clearer picture and some think, better game play.

Power ups during the '80s weren't something that Mario had access to. You had to use Mario's regular abilities to beat the obstacles and the bosses that stood in your way. There weren't any special mushrooms to make you grow, or spring blocks to help you jump higher while playing through the levels.

Super Mario Land gave Mario a more friendly look thanks to the increase in detail, and he took on a less sharp look and become a more lovable character as a result. This was a problem that the Game Boy Mario games were struggling with though. The limitations made it hard to give Mario all of the graphics they wanted too. The sprite that they created just wouldn't transfer from system to system well, so they had to come up with a better character creation for those that wanted Mario on a handheld Nintendo system.

Super Mario Land was a game that welcomed you to the world of Mario. With mushrooms, levels to beat and many obstacles that stood in your way, the players would have to make it through the land, beat the obstacles and the bosses and then rescue the princess. Thought of as just a regular guy, he didn't start getting many super powers until later on during the game development phase.

The next wave of Mario games is when the power-ups were first introduced. It's also when there were new focuses that would make the games go even further than they already have, with more objectives and complex level designs. This made a difference in the world of Mario and what was to follow.

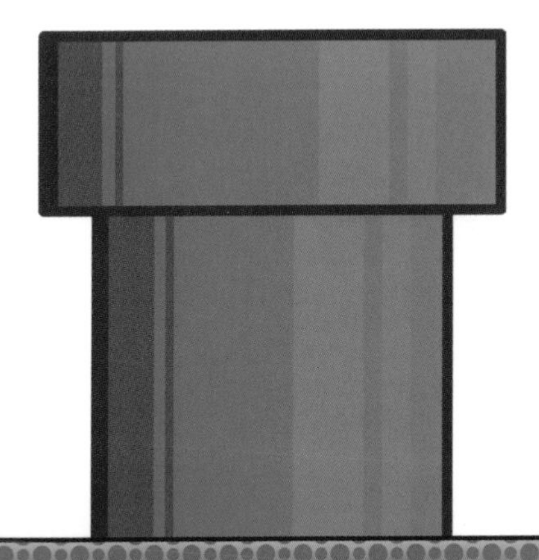

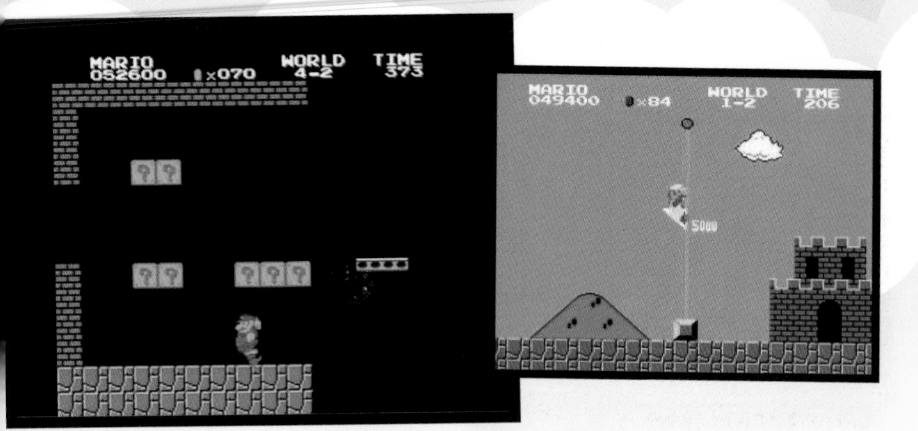

Though quite pixelated and not as smooth as the gaming consoles that you currently play on, Mario captured the hearts of gamers all over the world before personal gaming consoles even existed. That's pretty impressive if you ask us, and it's the reason that Mario has been able to persist as such a lovable character for all these years.

Mario continued on throughout the '90s showing up in a whole slew of games. The little plumber was the main character of many of these games, but also showed up as a side character in some as well. Keep reading to learn more about the '90s and Mario that would take over the world ahead.

Each of the games had its own challenges that kept players captivated, but with major advancements with each new gaming platform, the industry would continue to evolve the lovable character that everyone knows as Mario today.

As the '90s came, the '80s Mario quickly became outdated. Developers needed to act to keep the little guy fresh, interesting and something that players from future generations would want to experience. This led them to create new games, with more exciting objectives and to also make a new character that would change the face of Mario on TV screens all across the world.

MARIO OF THE 1990s

Moving Mario to the '90s was no easy task for the original developers. He had to be changed significantly to help him blend in with the new game-rich atmosphere with more capable game systems and better graphics. During this period of continual upgrades Mario became more detailed and better looking, but also came up against a whole new set of obstacles with new powers at his disposal. The '90s were a serious period of evolution for Mario, and the time that most features we know and love today came to be.

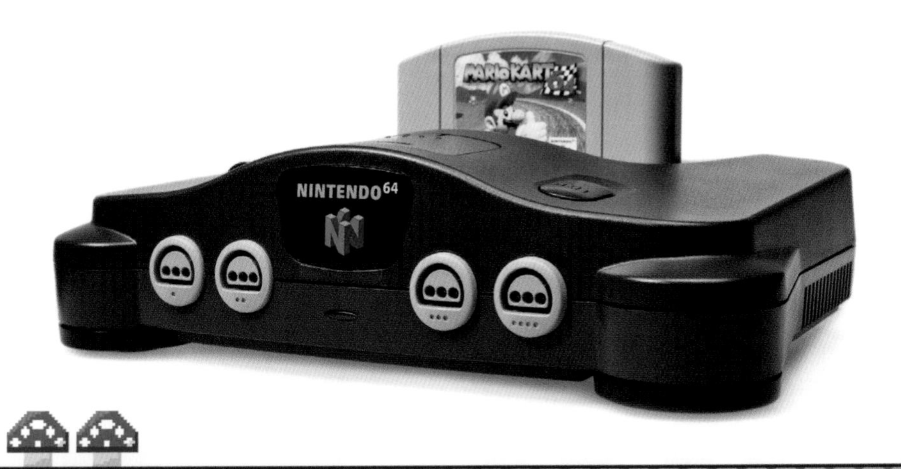

Walk with us and find out even more about gaming systems of the 90's and also the Mario games that were released to the public. These are more closely related to the Mario games that you know currently, making them a bit more relatable and fun.

GAMING CONSOLES OF THE '90S

Gaming consoles were plentiful in the '90s, and with those consoles came a whole new breed of characters, storylines and original games. Mario was among that mix of games and offered gaming entertainment in a big way for Nintendo.

The Super Nintendo Entertainment System (SNES) was one of the systems that bounced off of the original NES system developed in the '80s. It brought better graphics and smoother gameplay than the original. This made a huge difference in how many of the games, including Mario, were played on the system. The SNES was released in 1990, just in time to take the '90s by storm!

The Nintendo 64 was the next in line for Nintendo, and it was a revolutionary system with a built-in joystick and up to four players at a time on one screen. It was a huge upgrade that came out in 1996 and with it a whole new generation of Donkey Kong and Mario games as well. They were more widely available than ever before. The N64 was a gaming system that everyone had to have and it offered a whole collection of cool games, such as Star Fox, Metroid Prime, Zelda, and others that were not Mario related.

The Game Boy Color and Game Boy Pocket both came out towards the end of the '90s. The Color was in 1998 and the Pocket 1996. Both these systems allowed the user to play the games they wanted while on the go. The Game Boy Pocket didn't have color, but had clear graphics as compared to the original Game Boy. The Color was able to provide clearer graphics, that were also in color, which is something that was very big at the time.

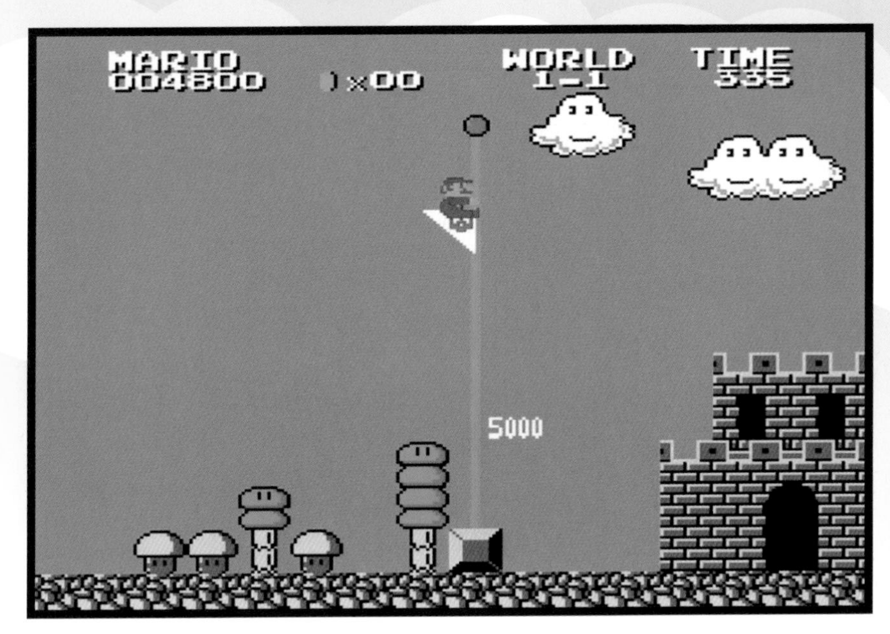

There were many Mario games that could be played and that came out during the 90's. Take a look at some of the biggest Mario games to be released in the '90s.

MARIO'S SPRITES CHANGED AGAIN

Mario's been evolving since the little guy served as Jump Man back in the early '80s, but the '90s were an especially exciting period for Mario. He became more colorful, more detailed and stopped looking like a little square and more like a little man. The developers found ways to make the games more enjoyable and life-like and that was a big deal for Mario fans.

Mario's sprite took on a different appearance. To create a more cartoon-like appearance, developers made use of the larger color palette available with new more powerful systems. Mario started to look more like a cartoon character you'd see on television and not one that was pixelated.

This was one of the largest differences that Mario of the '90s had to offer versus the little pixelated block man of the '80s. Mario had smoother graphics, better gameplay overall and definitely had more details than the previous versions.

SUPER MARIO WORLD

This is the first Mario game to ever be launched for Super Nintendo in 1991, but it was still a hit nonetheless. Princess Toadstool was once again kidnapped and the savvy Mario had to come out and defeat the bosses in order to save her from certain doom. The backdrop is in Dinosaur Land with many different playable zones, giving the player the control of where they'd like to play.

Some of the new lands that the players were able to take on included Yoshi's Island, Bridges, Star Land, Donut Plains, Vanilla Dome, Chocolate Island, Forest of Illusion and the Valley of Bowser, as well as a few others. This is also where you get to meet the newest Yoshi characters that come out more in the next few games.

One of the newest features for this game is the scrollable World Map, which wasn't in the previous games and gave users more control over their playing capabilities.

SUPER MARIO KART

Still a popular game today, Super Mario Kart has actually been around since 1992. This was the first ever racing game that was presented by Super Mario and it was one that quickly took off because all of the characters from Super Mario were featured in the racing.

Three different cups were proposed as the winning trophies for those that came in to take the lead. You could get the Mushroom, Flower and Star. Some even got to unlock a fourth trophy known as the Special Cup. The developers also added three different racing speeds and three different modes for those that wanted a bit more control over the racing that they did, as well as their playing experience levels.

One of the coolest parts of this racing game, besides that it was racing, was that the player could also choose the character that they wanted to speed with. All of the favorite Mario characters were there, such as Yoshi, Mario, Luigi, Donkey Kong Jr., Toad and even Bowser.

The sprites and karts in this racing game were not as advanced as more modern-day Mario Kart games, but they still were much better than the 80's Mario that so many have played with in the past.

SUPER MARIO RPG

Role Playing Games became more popular throughout the world, which meant that Mario had to step it up a bit and come out with a new game that he could be featured in, with a complete storyline. Coming out in 1996, Mario again took a turn to a new game and came with a new look.

Breaking away from the 2D track that so many have been playing before, a new wave of character came and went for this new game. Partnering with SquareSoft, Nintendo set out to make a new host of sprites to use in the game that would come with more 3D qualities.

The first ever Mario RPG game had a whole new storyline and it was released in Europe, where RPG games were becoming one of the biggest growing games in the industry.

MARIO GOING TOWARDS 3D

Mario has always had 2D capabilities and appearance. This is how the systems worked in the '80s and part of the '90s, and how they could render the graphics so smoothly. However, with the change in technology and the growing world around us, the need for a 3D model became greater. While he didn't completely go 3D, the new 2.25D gave Mario more dimension than he has ever had.

The new look was found in the Super Mario RPG: Legend of the Seven Stars for the Super Nintendo and then following with Wrecking Crew for the same system in 1998. This changed the way he looked, even if the previous games for the system still gave him a 2D appearance.

SUPER MARIO 64

First released in 1996 for the Nintendo 64 gaming console, Super Mario 64 put Mario back out there and brought him back to life after not being seen for a bit. This game gave players more, allowing them to try a whole new level with a more immersive world. Battling Bowser throughout different lands, Mario has to work to save Princess Peach this time.

Princess Peach is imprisoned and Mario has to go through over 100 star worlds in order to get to her and free her from the clutches of Bowser. He saves a new person with each level, getting him closer to the end of the game with each save that he makes. The levels do get a bit harder as you go along, but the main focus is to just get to Peach and be able to save her from the prison before it's too late.

With each new save, Mario collects power ups, hints, tricks and more from the appreciation of those that he saves. This early world not only showed that the gaming systems could handle larger, more intricate games but it also served as a template for a new world in the future of all Mario games.

While this is much different from the original games, it still had many of the qualities and characters that you would expect from a Mario game. It still ends with the appreciation of Princess Peach once he rescues her from Bowser.

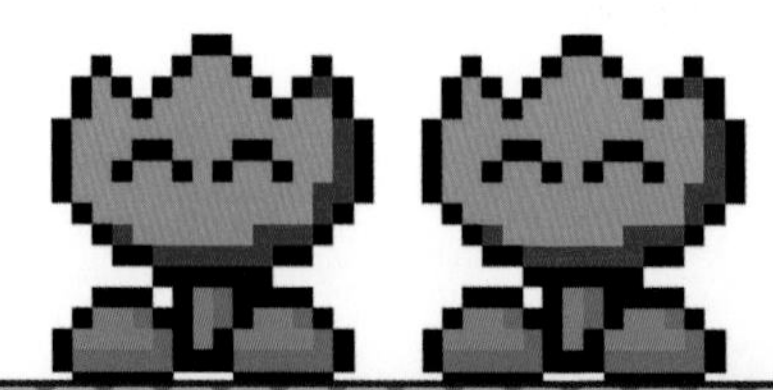

SUPER MARIO LAND 2

Originally released for the Game Boy systems, this game was a pocket version that allowed those that loved the first Super Mario Land that came out in 1989 to enjoy a second, more updated version. The game came out in 1992, making it one of the early Mario games from the 90's. Sometimes known as 6 Golden Coins, Mario had new obstacles to overcome in the battle.

Mario's evil twin Wario has raged against the world and Mario has to try to stop him before any more damage is done. He placed an evil spell across all of Mario Land and now the residents of the area think that Wario is the master and Mario is their enemy. This is a pretty different plot, but it is one that plays off of the original Super Mario Land.

In order to stop Wario and his evil plans, Mario has to find 6 Golden Coins that are hidden throughout each of the levels that the players have to play through. This will help him not only gain access back into his castle, but also break the spell and beat Wario. A bit different from the other games, but still just as fascinating. You have to be Mario and race against time to find all the hidden coins.

SUPER MARIO WORLD 2: YOSHI'S ISLAND

Released in 1995, this game made a storm within the Mario world by introducing little Yoshi and background of where he came from. Starting out as babies, both Luigi and Mario are carried by a stork over the sea. However, Luigi is then stolen by Magikoopa Kamek and Mario has to fight his way to find his brother.

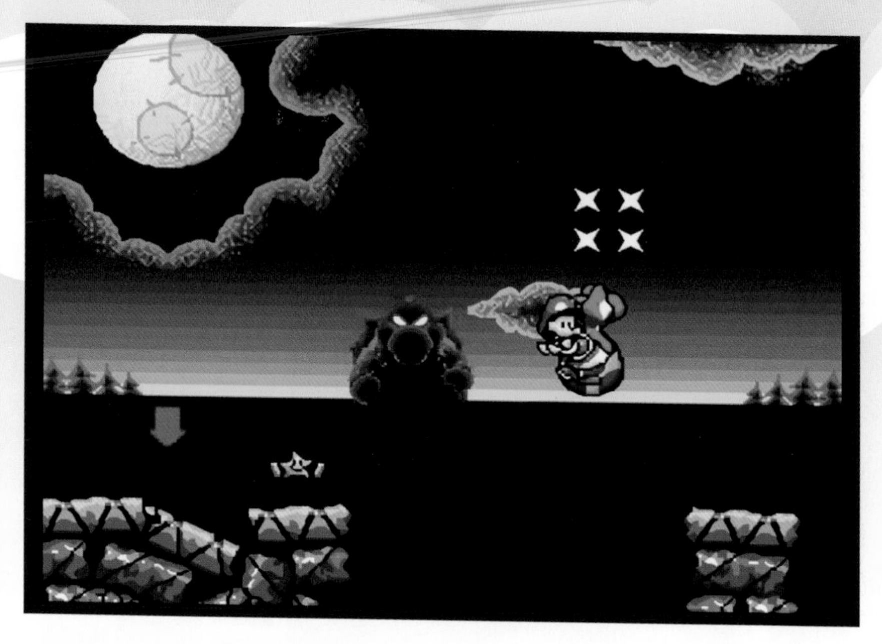

Dropped off at Yoshi's Island, home to the Yoshis, Mario has to become friends with these creatures and find a way to make it back to his brother before something bad happens to him. Journey through all of the levels and worlds of the game with the Yoshis by your side. Just a baby yourself, you have to go rescue baby Luigi from Kamek and Bowser, who are also both babies.

This was a different storyline than the others, but it provided a new world for players and also a different storyline they had to follow along with. This is where many of the Yoshis and their background came about, so you're able to get an idea of where the Yoshis all come from when you play this game.

The '90s brought a lot to the table in the world of Mario. With so many things happening at once, it was a great period to be a Mario fan.

Characters and storylines were continually changing and the games in the '90s gave fans more information about Mario and the other characters and the world they belong to.

Current Mario games continue to change and adapt with the new systems and technology, but these were a huge part childhood for so many children. Mario continued his evolution over the years, becoming more complex and advanced still to match the improving game systems.

Learn more about Mario and what the 2000s brought for him and systems that came out during those years. The Mario of yesterday is evolving more and more to be like the Mario that we know and love today.

1UP
000800
HI

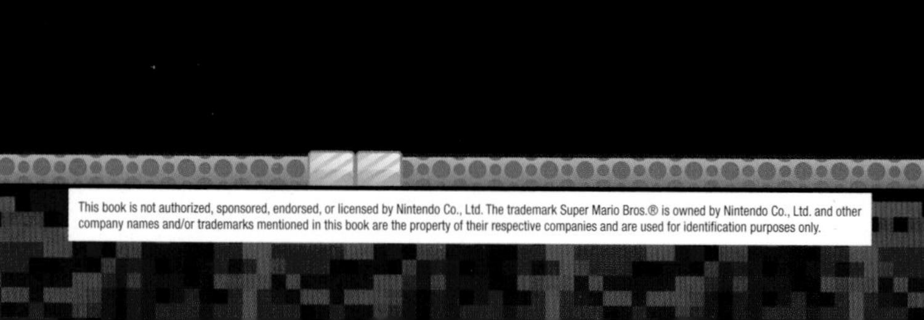

MARIO OF THE 2000s

Mario went on to expand his reach into different areas and gaming systems in the 2000s. His sprite also changed with him. Those cartoon characters started being more detailed, while also being able to do more within the games, since the technology of the time improved, the 2000s brought a lot of benefits to those that wanted a bit more Mario in their lives.

Learn more about the Mario that started in the new millenium and see where it has led us to this day. You may be surprised to know that he has come a very long way in the 2000s to get to the games that he is in now.

THE GAMING CONSOLES OF THE 2000S

With the 2000s brought a new wave of gaming systems. This meant for better gaming experiences for everyone that wanted enjoy something greater. With better graphics and smooth storylines, these systems easily took the world by storm.

The Game Boy Advance made a wave in the world of handheld devices. Coming to the market in 2001, many people wanted to grab one of these more advanced handheld devices. They provided a way to bring the game wherever you go, but also had colorful games that allowed you to play easily. Of course, there were many versions such as the SP or Micro that were later released, but each followed the same general concept of the Advance.

Another handheld console that hit the market was the Nintendo DS. It hit the market in 2004, with many more models to follow in the next few years after. The DS was also a big hit and provided users with a way to interact more intuitively by tapping or touching the bottom screen, while also using the top for viewing the games. Many of the DS versions soon followed after the original, such as the Lite and the DSi.

The Nintendo Game Cube came out in 2001, as a home gaming console following the N64. This also gained a lot of attention in the market since it supplied gamers with not only new games, but better graphics. The Game Cube was an updated version of the 64 that everyone wanted to have in their homes.

The Wii was another Nintendo game system that was released in the 2000s, coming out in 2006. This flew off the shelves at full force. It was a game system that allowed you to interact with the games that were in the console. It came with controllers much different from the normal game pads and paddles that gamers were used to using. It was an innovation in the gaming field that many other game makers had not yet reached.

MARIO'S SPRITE CHANGED FORM

With new game systems and new games came new looks for Mario that was once a little box guy with a hat and overalls. With so much more powerful machines capable of better graphics, the once hard to see character on the screen was now fully detailed and easily noticed within each of the games that he made an appearance on.

This was pretty much where the character stayed throughout the years. He has had some better graphics within the games, but overall, he is still the same Italian guy with a red hat, blue overalls and gloves. The mustache is here to stay as well, so check for it in any of the games that you come across.

SUPER MARIO SUNSHINE

The next major Mario game that was released and accepted throughout the USA was designed for the Gamecube. Initially, the game took a lot of backlash because the controller for the system did not work as well as the players had hoped it would, but with time, it ended up drawing people to the originality and need to learn something brand new.

Super Mario Sunshine was a novelty for Mario fans because it was different than what they were used to from Mario games. It forced fans to learn a new controller, and also to learn how to navigate an entirely new world.

This game also welcomes another bad version of Mario to it, Shadow Mario. Set to pollute the entire island where Mario and his friends are taking a vacation, Shadow Mario must be defeated in order to save the island and also the people that live on it. Mario is arrested for the crimes that Shadow Mario commits since they look the same, and that's how the game starts off.

One of the biggest additions to this game which wasn't shown in previous Mario games is the FLUDD. It is used to propel Mario into the air, promote clean up on the island and even work as an offensive tool if needed. Invented by Professor E. Gadd, he is able to use this tool for many different tasks that he comes across. Bowser Jr. is who Mario meets in the cleanup process.

Beat Bowser and be able to enjoy the rest of your vacation again once you collect Princess Peach, since he took her back with him to the castle. While there, the paintbrushes that the professor needs need to be collected. Many objectives and obstacles stand in your way, but this makes this Mario game much more enjoyable than older versions.

NEW SUPER MARIO BROS.

The New Super Mario Bros. was made to mimic the look and feel that the original Super Mario Bros. came out with. Much different from the other games on the market, this was meant to have that classic appeal but also have new upgrades that players already knew and loved when it came to playing Mario.

Bowser Jr. is back in this game and better than ever. He is ready to grab Princess Peach and hit the road again when it comes to taking her from Mario. Of course, he does and then Mario has to go through quests in eight different worlds to find her once again. Blending all of the old styles with the new, this was a game that hit the shelves hard and was able to deliver to those Mario fans!

SUPER MARIO GALAXY

Bringing together everything spacey, you're going to want to try out Mario in space with this awesome game. It was released in 2007, and a lot of those that love Mario wanted to follow along with this all new Mario game concept.

One of the most noted aspects of this Mario game was that it took a completely new direction. Bowser is of course in this one, but he made his castle go up in space, so it is out of reach for Mario to rescue the princess. Mario has to then travel through space and collect Power Stars in order to reach the princess. It is a bit different from the normal games, but definitely interesting.

With new puzzles and abilities, Mario could do much more than on some of the other Mario games out there. The game was a fresh take on the Mario franchise and many of the regular players loved the new feel. Super Mario Galaxy 2 was then presented shortly after the first. Bowser is seen as a giant in this one, Mario gets a spaceship and Princess Peach is kidnapped yet again. It is a regular Mario theme that has stood strong for so many years.

With the changes made throughout the years to Mario, you can expect that 2010 to this present day is going to bring it's own exciting flavor of Mario games with it. The next chapter is all the Mario games you know and love recently.

Walk with us and find out exactly what you can expect from the excitement that awaits you within the kingdom! Are you ready to rescue Princess Peach again?

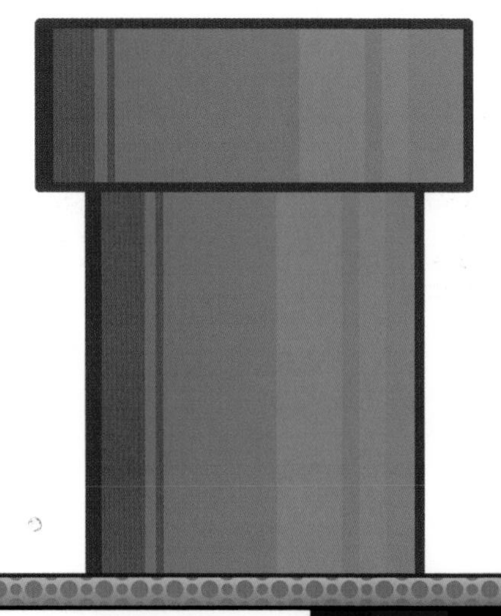

MARIO OF THE 2010s

Mario has changed in so many ways that those that were around when the first Mario came out are surprised by what the games now look like. With the changing games over time, Mario has definitely gotten more abilities, jumps to new heights (literally) and can now take on the bad guys that come to try and defeat him in new and exciting ways, even if it is mostly just Bowser.

Now you can rescue the princess in many different levels, modes and game backdrops. This is something that a lot of the Mario players of the world love to do today. If you're searching for a little bit more fun with Mario and his gang, then follow us and let us show you the coolest Mario-based features and games to come out between 2010 and today!

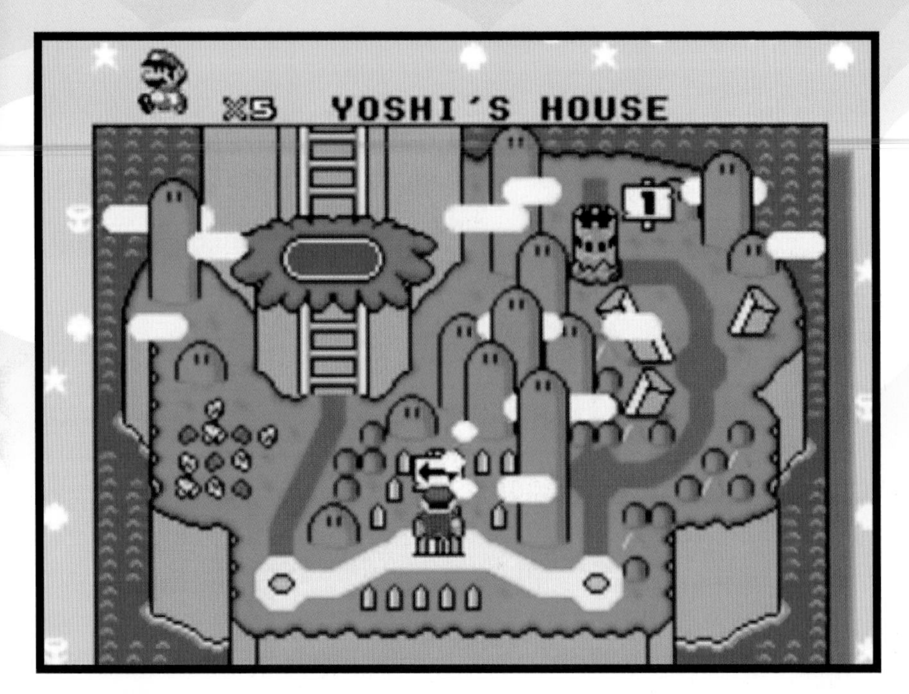

GAMING CONSOLES YOU ALL KNOW WELL

The consoles of this time didn't change too much compared to what was offered in the 2000s, they're basically more powerful systems with some cool new features added here and there. These consoles are perfect when it comes to playing a little Mario; just don't forget to throw in a little Star Fox every now and again, too.

The Wii U was one of the biggest gaming consoles to hit the market after the Wii and almost everyone wanted one these systems to play on. Providing the user with a way to play the Wii on your television screen like normal, but also the ability to pull it away from the screen using the large tablet controller, the game is right there in front of you even if someone else wants to use the television! Much like a small computer, this console is very different from the newer Xbox One and Playstation 4 released just a short while after the WiiU.

The Nintendo Switch is the next console after the Wii U and it's an even more novel concept entirely. It provides the user with a way to play right at home off the television or to bring the gaming with them wherever they go. One of the biggest advances throughout the gaming world, it's a console that gamers are lining up to get, especially the hardcore Nintendo fans out there. The system relies on a single portable system that connects to a television base for full-sized viewing at home, or slips out and accepts controllers at either side to create a gaming tablet for on-the-go. Easily switch between playing on the television and on the tablet-like device on-the-fly, making it easy to keep gaming no matter where you go.

MARIO'S SPRITE MADE A LEAP AND BOUND

Mario's sprite did not change too much between the 2000s to the 2010s. He might seem a bit different in each of the games that are presented throughout the years, but that is just dependent on the theme of the game, overall he still is around the same in terms of details.

NEW SUPER MARIO BROS. 2

Just like some of the other Mario games out there, this one was released in 2012 and it brings Mario on a chase to find Princess Peach once again. He has to collect the coins that are all scattered across Mushroom Kingdom. The Koopalings are in full force within this game, so keep an eye out for them.

Another version of this game was later released, New Super Mario Bros U. As one of the playable characters in Super Mario 3D World, he's just an average character. That's something that changes when it comes to the newest Super Mario Game, Odyssey.

SUPER MARIO 3D WORLD

Released in 2013, the gang ends up finding a fairy creature, known as a Sprixie. Bowser comes around, captures the creature himself and now the group has to go hunt down Bowser and save the Sprixie that he has taken. They enter into a whole new world, which opens up many different,options for the players. The new world is known as Sprixie Kingdom.

They have to find out what Bowser wants with the Sprixies and what makes them so special to where he took them. The graphics of this game have improved compared to the last few games, making it well worth the time you spend checking it out. One of the best games of the year, Super Mario 3D World was highly praised by Mario fans, critics and standard Nintendo players alike.

Keep in mind, over the years, there have been many, many different Mario games released. With everything from the Olympics to racing to anything and everything in between, there have been countless gaming options with the little Italian Plumber. The sports ones mostly did well on the gaming charts, and so did the racing ones on the Wii. If your favorite Mario-themed game isn't covered here it's still out there!

Play the Mario games you know and love and we encourage you to check them all out. Over time you just might build a unique collection of your own, that you want to come back to again and again.

Learn a bit more about Super Mario Odyssey and what you can expect from this game that's making every Mario fan excited with the possibility of something new and unique from Mario and his gang. Mario is able to do so much more in this game than you could ever imagine.

Check it out for yourself...

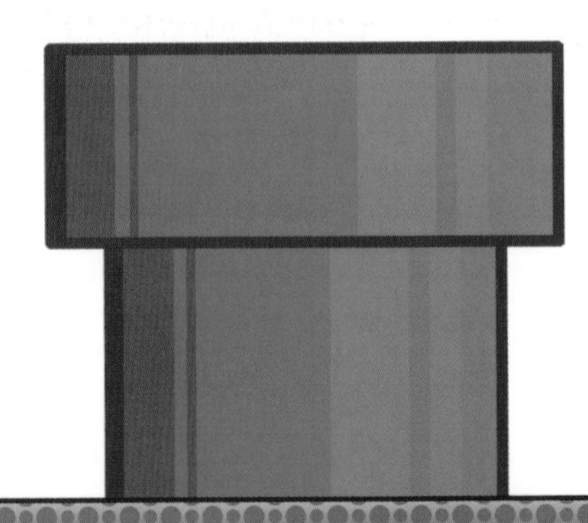

SUPER MARIO ODYSSEY STRATEGY

Mario never thought he would stray so far from home, but in an epic battle with Bowser over Princess Peach, he gets knocked out of the sky down to the Cap Kingdom in Bonneton. It's here that Mario befriends a bunch of new characters and he starts on a whole new epic mission. It's his job to stop Bowser and he won't have to do it alone.

The locals here are not only friendly, but they want to make sure that Bowser is stopped too! They are all ready to give Mario a hand at defeating him once and for all. Cappy, a friendly flying top hat wakes Mario to get him moving and to start working toward escaping Bowser's clutches once and for all.

So where does the Odyssey come from?
The incredible airship that Mario finds himself in command of is the Odyssey. He's able to travel between all of the kingdoms that are spread out throughout the world in search of Bowser. He will go to each of the lands in search of this villain, only to find himself fighting through level after level before accomplishing his goal. It's not an easy fight, but one that Mario is prepared to take on!

This all-in-one strategy guide will help you get where you need to go to locate Bowser and stop him from marrying Princess Peach. While you'll be working toward stopping Bowser throughout this game, it's all the places and experiences that you see along the way that will really hold your attention.

Put on your top hat and prepare for a bumpy ride because the Odyssey is taking on the biggest (and best) adventure it has ever known, are you ready for the ride to come?

It is up to Mario — and YOU! — to save the day and make sure Princess Peach is rescued in a timely manner... are you up for the challenge?

IMPORTANT THINGS, PLACES AND PEOPLE YOU'LL SEE

There are several items that you want to keep an eye out for while playing. Many of these things are going to come and go with each kingdom that you come across. Learn more about each of them and enjoy help getting through each kingdom, some additional points and a better shot at reaching Princess Peach.

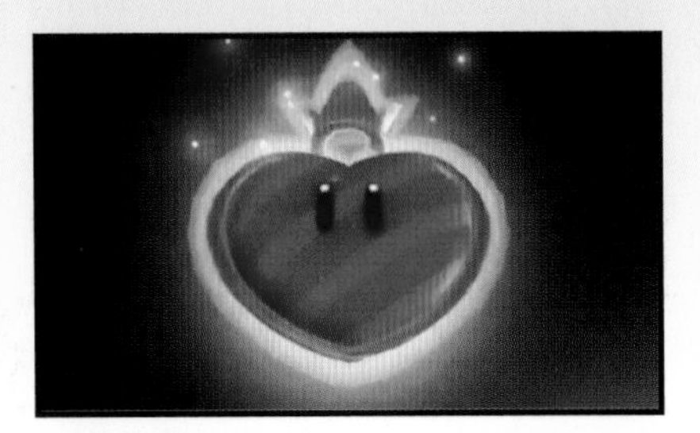

HEARTS

These are an important icon to watch out for. Mario's max health is indicated by the three hearts on the screen. Taking a hit will remove one heart and losing all three hearts results in a K.O. It will cost the player ten coins, but Mario will reappear at the closest check point if this does happen.

Picking up regular hearts can keep Mario's heart gauge topped up and help you avoid losing coins and time while working through the level. These are found by breaking blocks or pounding the ground in specific areas.

There are also special hearts in the game known as power-up hearts. These have a gold ring around them and are wearing a crown. This is a power-up that can make Mario's health bar go from three hearts to six! However, if you get knocked down to three or less, the power-up ends and Mario is back to his standard three hearts. These hearts are rare to find throughout the game, but they can also be purchased in Crazy Cap's shop or found when scanning Princess Peach's bridal amiibo. They're good to stock up on right before a particularly difficult level, so plan ahead!

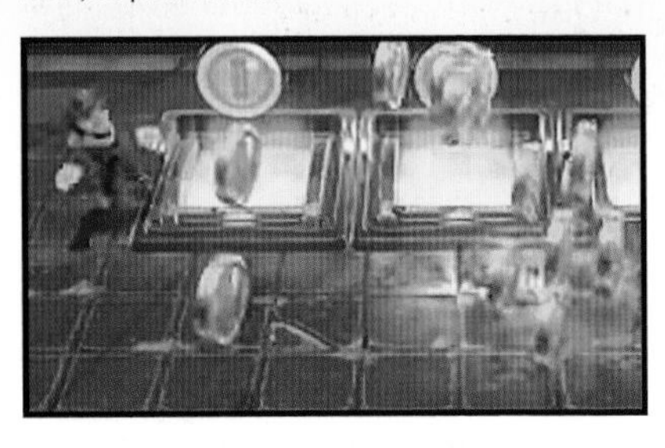

THE COINS

Gold coins are what Mario is going to have the most contact with as he goes through the game. They can be picked up and held onto. You can find them in busted blocks, in the ground and even by defeating the wildlife in the areas. By cracking the ground, Mario is then surrounded by a ring of coins that he can pick up.

When you see the gold coins, they can easily be picked up just by walking over top of them. Just keep in mind that if Mario is K.O.ed then he has to pay for his life back with ten coins. Collect as many as you can for this purpose, but also to spend in Crazy Cap's Shop and Hint Toad's Power Moon clues that he often has available if you have the right amount of gold coins to spend on the hints.

Single coins go right in your pocket, while coin blocks hold up to 10 coins, coin rings are three coins, Regional coins are two, Power Moon coins are five, picking up hearts while having full health brings five coins, and finally there are coin piles that offer sometimes very large amounts, but they offer different amounts depending on the pile.

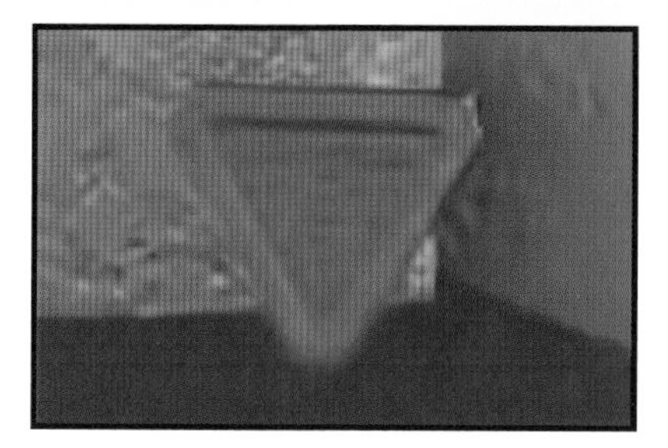

REGIONAL COINS

Regional coins are purple coins that are hidden throughout most kingdoms. They are the local currency and are somewhat rare to find. Usually the smaller kingdoms will give 50 coins throughout, while larger kingdoms give out 100.

These coins are useful as you can spend them within Crazy Cap's Shop when you'd like a unique item that can only be purchased through the use of the local currency for that kingdom. Hold onto all of the purple regional coins, as they're useful for specific purchases and for other purposes as well.

When the coins are collected, an outline will appear. Send either Cappy or Mario through the outline and you can collect two more gold coins.

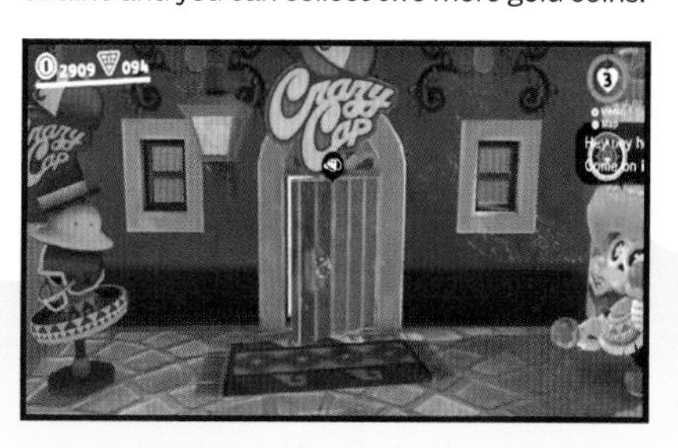

CRAZY CAP'S SHOP

Crazy Cap's Shop presents Mario with a wealth of items that can be purchased and used throughout the game. Both purple and gold coins are able to be spent inside the shop. Gold coins can be spent at any of these shops, while purple coins have to be spent in the kingdom that they were found. Each is shaped differently depending on the kingdom that they are picked up in.

You can only purchase some items within Crazy Cap's Shop with purple coins, so it is important to take note of how many you have as compared to how many certain items cost. By taking the time to locate all the local currency offered throughout a kingdom, you can afford to purchase all of the unique items the shop has in stock.

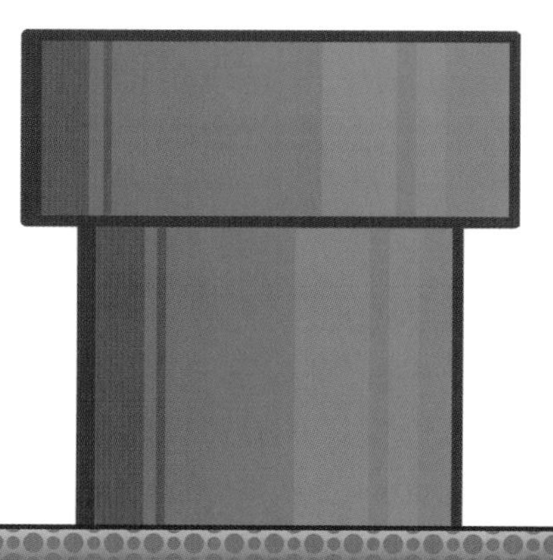

POWER MOONS

Mario's main goal is to find Bowser and to smack the stuffing out of him, but before he can do that and rescue his girlfriend he needs to gather enough Power Moons. Without those Power Moons travel isn't possible, so read on to learn exactly how you can track down the moons and get where you need to go.

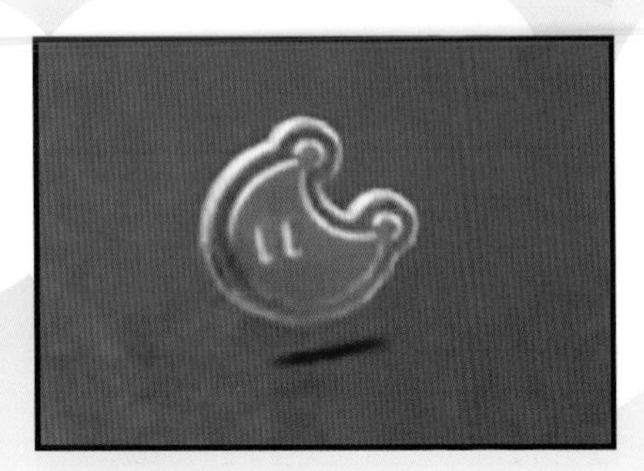

MOON SHARDS

Sometimes the Power Moons are broken up into moon shards. There are usually five smaller chunks that have to be found to be put together to make one. You have to gather all five of the shards to create one whole Power Moon. There is an indicator that shows how many shards you have and how many more you need. Once all five are collected, the whole Power Moon will be shown nearby for Mario to collect.

Picking up Power Moons can refill Mario's heart bar, while picking them up underwater can refill oxygen. This is extremely valuable to remember, because it allows you to continue hunting for strings of moons more easily. Additionally, once you grab the Power Moon, you still can go back to the area later on and go through the Moon's outline. This grants five coins and can also refill your hearts or oxygen again, so learning their locations will help you even after you have the moon.

When you visit each new kingdom for the first time, you're going to need to find Power Moons to replenish and repair the Odyssey airship. Different kingdoms require different numbers of Power Moons, so pay attention to how many you need so you know when you're able to move on. The number of Power Moons that are needed are shown in dotted outlines that will fill as you collect them. Additional to these Power Moons, you also have to complete a local quest before you're able to move to the next kingdom.

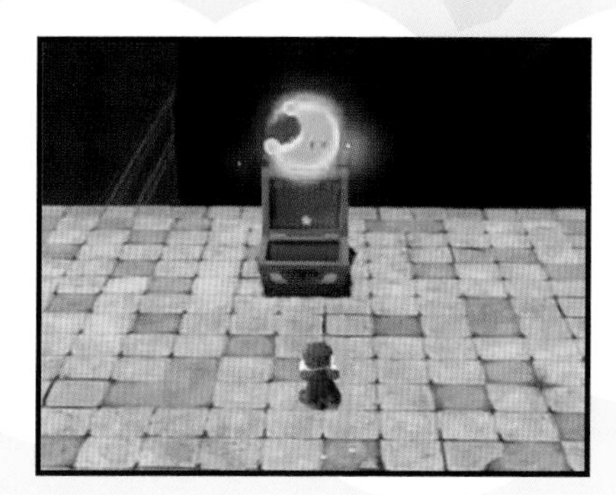

BURIED TREASURE

It wouldn't be a fun game without a little treasure hunt, would it?

Sure you'll find coins, Power Moons and hearts about in plain sight, but you're there's plenty of additional treasure buried down under the earth. Talkatoo provides pretty good hints for finding these hidden treasures in the ground, so listen closely.

Here are some other signs that there is hidden treasure nearby:

- Marks or cracks in the ground
- Glowing ground pieces
- Rumble from the controller when you're standing on a particular spot
- Mario sometimes gazes off to the spot where something is hidden
- Mario will toe the turf below him when something is amiss

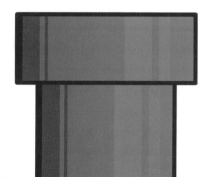

OTHER ITEMS OF NOTE

There are many other items that you want to be aware of when moving through each of the unique kingdoms. Each item awards the user with plenty of points, coins and other goodies, so take note so you know when you're looking at something important.

CAT MARIO AND PEACH

These are old-time pictures that are painted on some of the rock walls and other surfaces. When you find them, hitting Cat Mario with Cappy can award you with 10 coins, while hitting Cat Peach awards a heart.

BLOCKS

It just isn't a Mario game without blocks added to it. You're going to encounter a bunch of different blocks, so it's important to know what each one of them will reward you with.

Some of the blocks you cannot even see! They're invisible until something hits them. If you find something amiss around the sky area, then give a simple jump up and see if there is a block that has been hiding there all along.

Brick blocks are the norm for Mario games and they will be busted apart when Mario hits them, revealing coins or other tokens. Steel blocks can be used to hang on, jump on or jump from but they usually do not give anything, but are there to be used as a platform.

? blocks are those blocks that give off a decent amount of goodies. Once hit though, they turn into steel blocks that are no good anymore. They give out coins, hearts, Power Ups, Power Moons and much more. You never know what you're going to get until you hit them and see what they have to provide you with.

Keep in mind, some brick and ? blocks might not go to steel blocks right away. Keep hitting the blocks for additional coins and prizes. Once they become steel, then they have nothing more to give.

PIPES

Just like in the original Mario games before, pipes are found throughout many of the lands. By going into them, you can be transported to new places and see new people along the way. Just jump or walk in them and see where it takes you. Some of these hidden places bring you to places that award more coins, hearts or Power Moons.

CHECKPOINTS

Just like in the original Mario game, checkpoint flags are located throughout the kingdoms. With Bowsers flag on them initially, Mario can pull that down and put his own on it. They can be found by using the map or going through the entire kingdom.

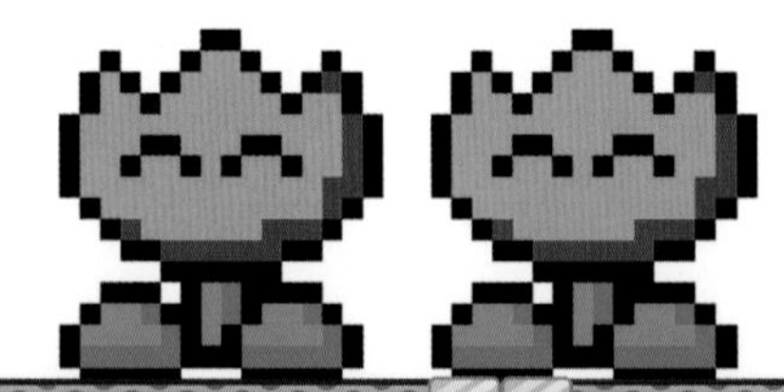

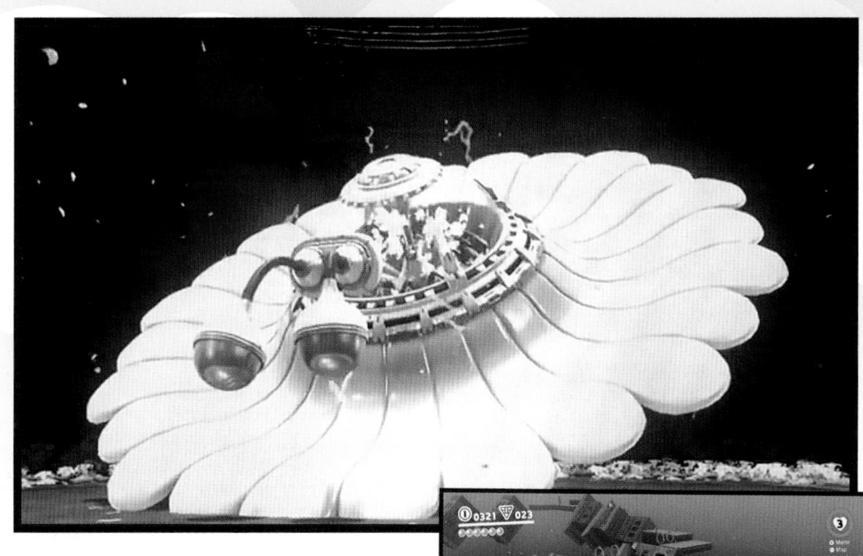

ROCKET FLOWERS

Throw Cappy at any of the rocket flowers in the game and have him throw them back. This turns into a nice rocket boost for Mario and he can run with the speed of light. Keep throwing the flowers at Cappy to keep the power up going.

P-SWITCHES

These provide the user with many different types of hidden effects. You might get blocks that you have to break for prizes, hidden vines that you can climb up for prizes or an assortment of other goodies that are waiting for you on the other side.

SCARECROWS

When you see scarecrows somewhere, they usually mean there is a timed challenge that is waiting for Mario. These platforms only appear when the challenge is activated. Place Cappy on the scarecrow during the challenge. Mario has to complete all of the tasks on his own while Cappy is sitting on the scarecrow's head.

Mustache man, you're back!

HAT TRAMPOLINE AND LAUNCHER

The hat trampoline opens up when Cappy is thrown onto it, allowing Mario to propel himself higher or further. However, the launcher allows Cappy to be thrown a far distance, collecting coins and hearts as he goes. The launcher looks like two wheels on a triangle, while the trampoline looks like a flower that is closed until Cappy is thrown at it and then it opens.

PULSE BEAMS

Pulse Beams can be dangerous and you can be sure that if they're lit up, something around has activated them. These blocks are never just sitting around, and you need to be careful when in the presence of them. There are usually a handful in one place at any given moment. The expanding waves from these beams must be avoided, as they can take out bricks, blocks, wildlife and anything that stands in their way. They're tricky to jump over so be cautious when moving about an area when you see the beams.

KINGDOM LOCALS

Each area has its own set of locals, all different from the next. Speaking with them and learning more about the area is key to finding the Power Moons that are hidden within each of the kingdoms. Crazy Cap's Shop is usually located where all of the locals are, as well as locals that are in need of Mario's help. Complete the quests and become the hero.

Uncle amiibo
If you happen to have some, put 'em to work! They're good at finding any stray Power Moons.

TALKATOO

This feathered bird is a delight when you seek answers. He's found in each of the kingdoms perched atop a tree. He gives Power Moon clues by their names, allowing Mario to find some of them with ease. He can give up to three names of Power Moons at a time, which means you can go back and ask him for further clues on others once the first three have been found.

HINT TOAD

Another creature within the kingdoms that gives tips and tricks, this toad usually hangs out near Uncle Amiibo. He gives Power Moon finding hints to make the adventure a bit easier. However, his tips do not come without a price. You will have to pay Toad 50 coins for hints finding some of the most hidden Power Moons throughout the kingdoms.

UNCLE AMIIBO

When Hint Toad begins scouting, he brings along Uncle Amiibo. He uses his special power to help locate Power Moons that are hidden in each kingdom. You can actually use this amiibo to get a free Hint Toad tip! However, this function can only be used every few minutes, so you will have to wait a bit before getting another hint.

CAP KINGDOM

BONNETON

You start the game in Cap Kingdom, where Mario lands after being pushed into the sky by Bowser. There are plenty of features and locations to take note of while in this cheerful place where many new friends can be found.

GETTING THROUGH CAP KINGDOM

Mario has to go through a series of steps to move onto the next kingdom. Here are some of the challenges he is going to come up against in his journey.

Team up with Cappy, who's sister Tiara was stolen along with Princess Peach by Bowser. Together, you will both go through the kingdoms and beat the quests that you come into contact with.

TO THE TOP OF TOP-HAT TOWER

All of the airships throughout Bonneton were destroyed by Bowser, so now Mario and Cappy have to come up with a way to make it across all of the kingdoms and get to where Bowser is. Cappy knows where there is an old airship and he thinks they can get it running.

Throwing Cappy against the wooden posts and towards enemies helps Mario collect coins along the way. It's an important skill to master, so make sure you're tossing Cappy around often. Toss Cappy at enemies and other wild creatures alike and you can take control of them, as well. Once in your power, you can use their special abilities (the frog provides high jumping capabilities) to make it through the rest of the level.

DEFEATING THE BOSS TOPPER

In order to get to the aircraft, Cappy and Mario have to defeat the boss that is waiting for them at the top of the tower. Topper is his name and he is quite angry that you have come to take the last aircraft. Topper will attack by using the three top hats that he is wearing. Once the attack starts, use Cappy to knock down the top hats from his head one by one so that he is unable to fight effectively. Mario can then leap up on his head. Once all of the top hats are knocked off, you have to go through the process all over again to win.

A Spark Pylon will appear once Topper has been beaten. Toss Cappy to capture it and then zip along the wire to the next kingdom.

- There are four regional coins high on a wall in the Frog Pond location. There are three more in Top-Hat Tower and three more in the poison peril area.
- Cap Kingdom also has 31 Power Moons hidden throughout, some of them can only be obtained after defeating Bowser. Hint: Bonneter Blockade, the Frog Pond and the Poison Tide.

CASCADE KINGDOM

FOSSIL FALLS

The next kingdom you're going to find yourself venturing to is Cascade Kingdom. With many naturalistic sites to see, it's easy to enjoy the looks of this kingdom, but make sure you look closely at your surroundings. Take note of some of the awesome places there is to see, search carefully for treasure and don't forget to collect those Power Moons.

THE STEPS TAKEN IN CASCADE KINGDOM

Of course, Mario needs to get to the princess and save her, but he can't do that without going through the necessary quests in Cascade Kingdom. In order for Cappy and Mario to get further in their journey, they're going to need an aircraft and not just the electrical wire that they got here with.

This means that finding Power Moons should be priority when going through this world, of course those hearts, coins and extras are also nice to find along the way.

GOING ATOP THE FALLS

In order to get as many moons as possible to power the aircraft, Mario will have to go atop the falls to reach many of them and beat the boss for this level. After exploring the falls Mario needs to move on to the next stage, but there's a well standing in his way! To get through it take control of the Big Chain Chomp and smash right through it! Cappy is the key to making this happen.

Getting through the wall is just the beginning through. Once you break through that wall, you're going to have to walk through the Ancient Wall and go through paths and warp pipes to finally make it to the boss level. You'll have an opportunity to find a hidden Power Moon while venturing through the tunnels here, so keep your eyes open.

MADAME BROODE

At the end of the level, you're going to come across the boss's lair. Here you'll have to take on Madame Broode. She will prove a real challenge, but you have what it takes to overcome this tough boss, don't you?

While battling Madame Broode, pay close attention to the golden chain chompkins on a leash. This massive pet will determine whether you are successful or you fail. Follow the golden arrows on the ground and dodge out of the way when the chompkins come towards you. Throw Cappy at the petto knock it's hat off and then again to capture it. Once captured, you can put the chompkins to work fighting Madame Broode for you and that's when you'll make real progress.

Defeat her pet three times and you win and also get another Power Moon for your aircraft.

- During a boss battle, check into the rocks. Break them open and Mario can usually find hearts hidden within, if he needs the extra help.
- 50 regional coins are located throughout this kingdom. You can find some of them atop a cliff, behind a red door and on the ledge of the 8-bit level.
- There are 40 Power Moons located throughout the kingdom, one you have to beat the boss for, some of the others are hidden in fossilized rocks, in a dinosaur nest, and in the secret path to fossil falls.

SAND KINGDOM

TOSTARENA

Once you've gone through Cascade Kingdom, it is time to travel forward and take on the next challenge in Mario's quest. That challenge can be found in the town of Tostarena. It's a colorful, welcoming town with new friendly faces, new monsters to battle and of course more new Power Moons and coins to gather!

JAXI RIDES

Unlike Taxi rides that we all know so well, the inhabitants of this kingdom rely on Jaxi rides to get them where they need to go Explore the desert in comfort and style when you take one of them out for a stroll.

COMPLETING THE QUESTS IN SAND KINGDOM

Of course, Mario needs Power Moons from the Sand Kingdom as well, and he's going to have to work hard to get them. Mario must move through the kingdom in search of Moons, as well as coins, hearts and other hidden treasures. With an itinerary set, make sure to go through each of the following steps for success in the Sand Kingdom.

THE HIGHEST TOWER

Once again it's up to Mario to journey to the highest point of the Kingdom to get farther in the quest line. You'll be tasked with located and scaling the tallest tower in the region, so prepare for some tough work. On the way you'll also notice that Bowser's giant footprints are in the sand along the route you need to travel. You're getting closer!

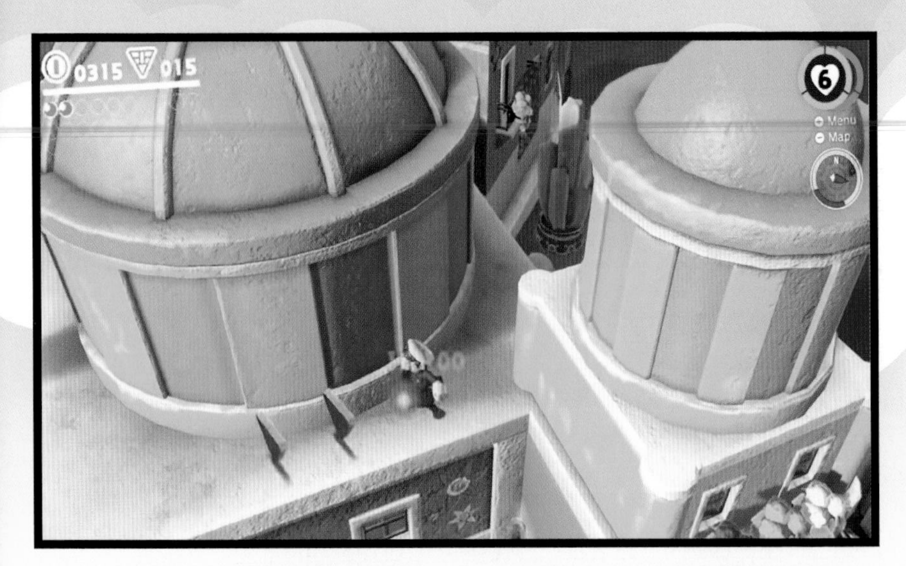

Go to the Tostarena Ruins Entrance and make your way up the stairs to the top. Note: To have Cappy come back sooner while moving around, just shake the controller and he will fly right back, so you can throw him again as you journey onward and upward.

While moving through this level you'll encounter tough Bullet Bill characters. To deal with them, you just have to capture them. This is the safest way to ensure that you can make it through the level. Fly the Bullet Bill through the rings, release them and then leap onto the platforms ahead.

Don't worry so much about searching for Power Moons while going through this level, you just need to focus on beating the level first because it's difficult. Dodge, dunk and use the flower launcher to make it through the twisting and turning hallways you have to follow through. Look for three crates towards the end of the level. Each will have something different inside of them: binoculars, a Power Moon and then a surprise.

You need patience and speed for this level, you'll have to move quickly and know when to dodge for success. Keep practicing and you'll get it with time.

BOTTOMLESS CANYONS

In this level you'll find a world underneath a world. With mountains of sand under the kingdom, you will go here to find Moon shards, but also regional coins that are left about. You may have to do some digging, but each of them can be found hidden below the levels of the kingdom above. You'll have to fight to get onto the platform that will bring you down, but throwing Cappy helps you get there easier.

You get a freebie right next to the Moe-Eye when you first enter, but from there, you have to search for the other shards. You can collect Moe-Eyes to use during this hunt, as well because their special sunglasses help them see things that are otherwise invisible to the naked eye.

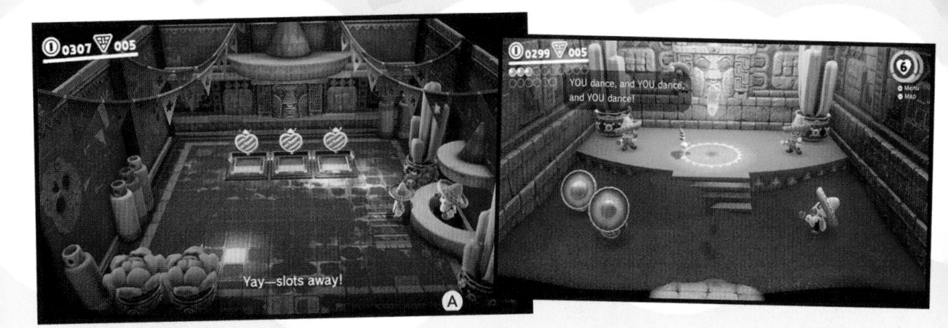

INVERTED PYRAMID SHOWDOWN

If you're looking for a good fight in this level, you're in for a treat! Roll across the desert and enter into the inverted pyramid to see what is waiting for you there. You'll have to go through the 8-bit level in order to come out at the end for the final boss to defeat.

Keep an eye out for a large crack in the wall while working your way through the pyramid. This is where one of the Power Moons is hidden and you can easily break the wall to collect your prize.

Hariet is the boss of this level and she's not to be taken lightly. Between her hat and her ponytail she has a variety of special moves to use on you. She uses her hat to attack and her ponytail to throw bombs at you. If you can stay on one side of the arena and dodge the bombs, or use Cappy to knock them back towards her, then you can keep yourself alive while working on a strategy to take her out. If the bombs hit you or the floor in front of you, this can mean K.O.

She will continue to come at you with her hat and bombs, so step lightly and move around as needed throughout the fight. As time moves forward, Hariet will zig zag in front of you to make it harder and harder to get ahead of her. All you have to do is jump on top of her head and she will be defeated. Do that and you'll be awarded with another sweet, sweet Power Moon.

THE HOLE LEFT BEHIND

Once you beat the boss, you'll be amazed by what the pyramid does. It actually lifts up and takes off leaving behind a massive hole in the ground. Mario has to go into in order to finish his quest. However, before heading down into the deep dark abyss, make sure that you have all the Power Moons as well as any goods from the store you think you'll need. You don't know what awaits you inside.

The hole actually leads to an icy wonderland where you will meet yet another boss, once you make your way through the maze that they laid out for you. You have to use Cappy on the launcher in order to break the ice blocks overhead to make it through the maze.

Capture a Goomba to give you more traction while walking on the ice. They can sometimes slip, but it is less likely if you have one in your control.

If you continue through the maze, you will come across a Power Moon laid out for you as well as regional coins just behind it. The Binding Ring

was once placed in this area, but it's currently out of place because Bowser took it. There is just a a bleak shadow left behind.

To get to the next boss at this point, capture a Bullet Bill and ride it across the gap.

KNUCKLOTEC

The boss that comes and meets you at the end of this icy level is Knucklotec. When he enters the room, he slams the floor and sends icicles raining down to the ground, some of them smashing open holding hearts. Notice where these are before the fight.

During the fight Mario will encounter flying fists. Watching for the shadows can help you dodge each one as it is sent next to you. It's important to also watch out for the falling icicles each time he smashes down on the ground because they're deadly and will quickly take you out of the fight if you aren't careful.

Dodge the fists and the icicles a few times and then you'll have your moment to strike! Knucklotec will grabe you with his hands, it's now that you need to break free and then capture one of his hands to use against himself.Use Cappy to do this and once you do, he will be defeated. He also leaves behind a Power Moon.

If you defeat the boss but you're still stuck in the kingdom, you'll have to go back through hthe levels to search for all the other Power Moons that you left behind.

- There are 100 regional coins throughout Sand Kingdom. Some of them can be found along the way to meet the bosses.
- Look for 89 Power Moons all hidden or held throughout the kingdom. Check the ruins, leaning pillars, luggage, fountains and dunes to find some of them.

LAKE KINGDOM

LAKE LAMODE

Choosing Lake Kingdom connects the paths that Mario needs to follow in order to get to Princess Peach. In this area you'll discover plenty of mysteries and wonders, as well as meet new people along the way.

THE JOURNEY IN LAKE KINGDOM

Mario must go through a series of steps here in order to make it to the end. While working through this kingdom, just like all the others your priority should be on tracking down the Power Moons and on beating the bosses that will challenge you along the way.

Upon landing, the stairs are broken going into the Water Plaza, so Mario has to find another way in. It is possible to triple jump from the beach, toss Cappy to the top of the wall and then tackle jump up the landing. However, it can be a difficult move to master.

Cross over the water near where the ship landed. Bounce off the trampoline and bounce over the gates. Grab the coins that pop up and then grab the zipper and tug. This creates an opening for Mario to go through.

Make sure to stay lined up with the air bubbles ahead, collect the regional coins as you make your way through the path then take a right at the first fork that you come across. Collect the Power Moon from the treasure chest and you're in!

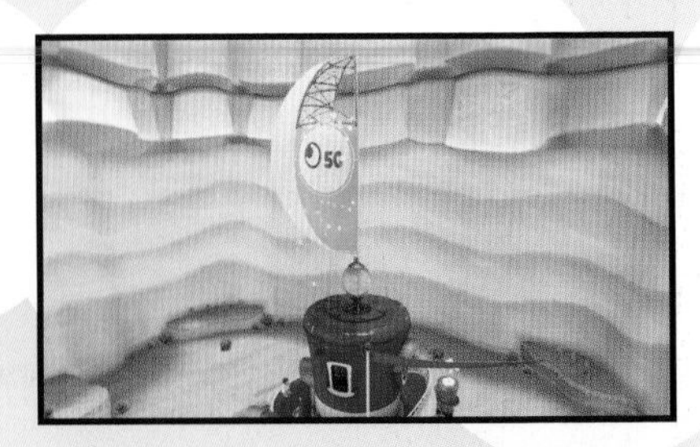

Make sure that you keep in mind that while Mario can swim under water he only has a limited supply of air!. The meter on the side tells you when he is running out of air, so keep your eye on it and prepare to grab bubbles as needed. If anything, capturing a Cheep Cheep can give Mario a Power Up to breathe even longer while under water.

Swim through the rest of the maze under water and collect the Power Moons as you go. Make sure to stop and collect standard and regional coins along the way. You may have to break through some of the entrances in order to keep going. There are also five shards hidden along the way, so keep an eye out for those as you swim along.

One of the Power Moons that you will come to notice is on the back of Dorrie. Dorrie is extremely peaceful and she will let you take the Moon right off her back without a problem, so be nice to her.

WATER PLAZA LOWER LEVEL

The lower level of the Water Plaza welcomes you a sprawl of coins to gather up, you'll be raring to head to the item shop after a trip through here! Travel through the watery hallway to the left to go to the middle level of the plaza. There is a P-Switch there that you can hit to open the doorway and allow yourself entry into the room. Once there, you can lower down the trampolines, making it much easier to jump and reach the crates along the top.. This is where another Power Moon is hidden.

Follow along with all of the following steps to make it through the kingdom and onto the next.

RANGO THE BOSS

Rango is a vicious boss equipped with a buzzsaw hat atop his head. He'll cut you apart with this aggressive hat if you aren't careful. During the fight make sure to stay out of range of the hat, and pay close attention to learn how Rango moves around. When he goes to throw his hat , throw Cappy at it and then bounce on the underside of the hat, which turns into a trampoline. Bounce on top of Rango's head and collect the Power Moon he drops after you bop him three times.

- 50 Regional coins are hidden throughout the kingdom, the red door has some behind it and the crack in the wall makes way for others.
- There are 42 Power Moons hidden throughout the kingdom, some of them are hidden and others are out in plain site. Check the hidden passages, bodies of swimming water, secret zippers and cliffside to uncover each and every one of the hidden moons.

WOODED KINGDOM

STEAM GARDENS

Steam Gardens is a factory location within the Wooded Kingdom and it's the site for most of the Power Moons as well. Keep your eyes open and look around for all the hidden objects that you have to find while going through this level.

TAKING ON THE PATH AHEAD IN THE WOODED KINGDOM

Mario starts off his journey in the Wooded Kingdom at the southern reaches of the region. From there he has to move through all the challenges ahead, gather up the Power Moons and get all the power necessary to get the ship moving once again. It will prove a more difficult task than expected though, so buckle up and prepare for as serious fight!

THE DIRT PATH LEADS YOU ON

After making it through the Southern Reaches, follow along with the dirt path and buy as many Power Moons as possible from the Cap Shop along the way. Use the dirt path to travel to the Sphinx. Once you encounter the Sphinx it's up to you to give him the correct answer. Bowser wants flowers — once you do that you can move on to the Iron Road.

- Collect the regional coins that are atop the outer wall of the kingdom. Make sure to look up, as they're always hiding in this area.
- Orange and yellow blocks on the pathway will collapse under Mario's weight, so make sure to step lively now!

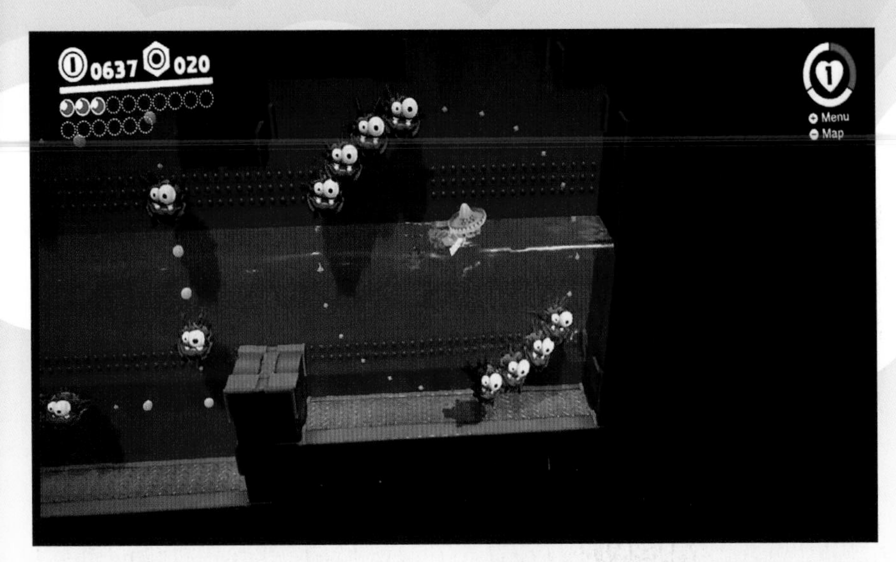

While walking down the Iron Road, stay on the path and avoid waking the angry T-Rex that's napping away peacefully on the road. Your quest is to take the seeds from the gardener and plant them in the pots that are found at the end of the path.

Toss Cappy at the purple poison, as well as the plant that spits it out to reduce your chances of getting hit with this stuff. It could come with bad results if you do! As long as you make careful use of Cappy along this road you should have no trouble moving on without getting poisoned and planting the seeds along the way. Make sure to use the ledges and other items to hop over the unsteady boards and get to the destination quickly.

This is one of the most complex levels that Mario is going to go through, so it is important to activate the Warp Flags each time you notice one. The flags are important markers that will help you avoid getting lost and keep you in the correct world the entire time.

FIGHT THE BIG POISON PIRANHA PLANT

In this fight it's up to you to best the massive man-eating plant. To do this toss Cappy at the rocks along the sides of the ledges to knock them down. You'll knock down a bunch that you can throw at the plant monster to stun it. Once you do that get as close as you can by throwing more rocks thorugh Cappy and then jumping up on top of the plant head. Do this successfully a few times and you'll beat the plant and get rewarded with a Power Moon.

THE FLOWER THIEVES ABOUND

The next takes you through a glass chamber that shatters, making way to a P-Switch. Before you jump on it, find the gap in the ground and jump down there. While you're down there capture an Uproot, this will help you climb across the wall effectively. Go around the corner and up over the ledge. If you go to the proper spot you'll locate another Power Moon.

Step on the switch and a giant flower will bloom before you. Once it blooms follow along with the pathway that appears. Just make sure to go fast, as the flower does not last for long. Do the same thing when you get to the next flower.

Hit the P-Switch inside the tower and then follow the road you gain access to. Capture an Uproot to get a life heart that is hanging on the side of the wall. Stretch the Uproots legs to reach the P-Switch above you. Crack open the nut that appears when walking through the path and you will find another Power Moon. Follow it the path to the very top.

The flower road that you follow changes with time, and disappears and reappears at timed intervals. While climbing up the spiral staircase, make sure to jump on the shadow because there's another Power Moon up there.

SPEWART IS THE NEXT BOSS

When you walk outside on the top of the pathway, you will come face to face with Spewart. As his name suggests, this character spews poison out everywhere, leaving you with a very difficult fight. Make use of Cappy to clean up the poison each time he spews it out, then toss Cappy right at Spewart and jump up above him and ground pound him.

Once he is rolling around on the ground, throw Cappy at him again to knock his hat off. When his hat's off ground pound him one more time to finish him off. You'll easily defeat him with this strategy and he'll drop another valuable Power Moon. Now you're one step closer to making it through the Kingdom and getting to the princess.

THERE ARE VISITORS IN THE SECRET FLOWER FIELD

Earlier a flying object was spotted landing in the Secret Flower Field. Now it's up to Mario to to go find out who these new visitors are. Take some time to go through the level up above to collect all the standard and regional coins, and the Power Moons, then go back down to the field to check out the new visitors that await.

Torkdrift is the one that has landed and he's looking for information about the area. To best this new boss you'll need help from an Uproot, so capture the creature before you get into the fight. Once you do, you can extend his legs and place pressure on the bulb that is coming from the aircraft. Crack it like you would with one of the nuts.

Mario has to do the same on the three cubes that appear, as these are what is giving Torkdrift his power. Crack each of them while on the move, to avoid getting hit with any of the lasers that Torkdrift shoots out during the battle.

Use the Uproot to break all the cubes, then head back to the dome to crack that. Once you complete this step you've bested Torkdrift and you'll be rewarded with yet another Power Moon.

- The Wooded Kingdom has 100 regional coins scattered throughout the region, some of them can be found in Sky Garden Tower or in the trunks of trees throughout the forest.
- There are 54 Power Moons placed throughout this Kingdom. Many of them are given after quests, but you can find them as you go along too. Some are invisible, so it is good to look around for shadows. Always check in rock cracks along the way to avoid missing moons!

CLOUD KINGDOM

NIMBUS ARENA

Along his travels Mario can't help but stop in the location where happiness comes to life, the Cloud Kingdom. Up here is where the Doves live, and their home is known for tranquility and beauty, but there are going to be some real challenges for you here as well. Everyone that visits the Cloud Kingdom decides that they want to move there, and for good reason; it's irresistible!

COME FACE TO FACE WITH BOWSER

Congratulations! You've caught back up with Bowser in one of the most peaceful looking locations in all of the Mario Universe, but you have your most intense fight yet to deal with. It's time to take Bowser on hat-to-hat so get ready for a serious battle.

When Bowser jumps on the platform, he means business. He'll tosss his hat at you, and it's designed to deliver a series of punches when it gets close enough. Be smart and counter the hat with Cappy to keep it from doing damage. A proper throw with Cappy will knock Bowser's hat upside down, letting you claim it for yourself.

Put on the hat and k now that some extra powers await you when you do. Once wearing the hat you'll be able to move through the rings of fire unharmed, and you need to run after him when he tries to get away. Once Bowser grows tired, use his own hat against him with as many hits as you can get in. Bowser's hat will knock him out and you've won the first battle! Unfortunately it's not the only one you'll face.

Once Bowser wakes back up he's tougher than ever before. He has two purple hats to attack with now and they can do serious damage if you aren't careful. The strategy is different this time though. You shouldn't throw Cappy at the purple hats, but at the white hat atop Bowser's head. Hit the white hat and the purples will be removed. Once you do this Bowser will run once again and you must chase him and attack just as before. This concludes round two!

- There are 9 Power Moons here, but you must come back to get them after you have gone through other kingdoms.

LOST KINGDOM

FORGOTTEN ISLE

This is a run down place that holds a lot of mysteries. It's up to you to uncover the mysteries of this ancient place on your own if you want to make it to the next kingdoms. Go through the area with care, and prepare for the challenges that await on your way to Princess Peach.

MARIO HAS A QUEST TO TAKE ON!

Mario faces some serious challenges in the Lost Kingdom so prepare to work hard and overcome each one that comes your way. It won't always be easy, but it's worth the effort I promise!

RESCUE CAPPY!

Klepto has come around and swooped up Cappy! It's up to you to get him back. The snatch happens when you're headed north towards the bridge. Klepto swoops down and snags Cappy right off your head and heads towards Swamp Hill! You'll have to travel there and get him back, but take care, because the going is much tougher without Cappy to aid you.

Advance to the ruins that have the strange starburst shapes on them. Go to the side and pound on one of the starburst. One side will raise, while the other falls and then pounding again creates a teeter-totter effect. Keep climbing up and using the starburst as you go. Travel up to the top of the stairs — this is where Cappy is being held.

Patiently wait for the wigglers to make their way past, and be careful not to engage them, without Cappy they'll prove very difficult enemies. Once you do, run up the stairs and make Klepto follow you back down. Once he is on one side of the ruins, hit the starburst which will fling Klepto up into the air — making him drop Cappy so you can grab him and keep going.

COLLECT ALL THE POWER MOONS YOU NEED

Now that you have Cappy back—congratulations about that by the way!—it's time to start on your next mission. It's one that involves Power Moons, so prepare for a bit of treasure hunting. You'll have to journey around the kingdom and seek out each and every one of those Power Moons until you have enough to continue traveling. This takes some time so be patient.

Of course, keep a close eye out for Klepto during your search, as he likes picking up treasure and grabbing them up whenever he can and might take Cappy again!

- This level has 35 Power Moons hidden throughout. Make sure that you check below the cliff's edge, in the caves, in the rock ledges and even in with the butterfly's you find along the way.
- The region also has 50 regional coins to find. Some of them are hidden by the Power Moons and others are found in other areas. Make sure you look up high everywhere you go!

METRO KINGDOM

NEW DONK CITY

This city looks just like a city when you land there, so don't be surprised at the sight of some serious sky scrapers. There is a lot to see and do and Mario will have his hands full trying to get through this level with all the quests and Power Moons that he needs to collect.

MARIO TAKES ON THE CITY AHEAD

Mario needs 20 Power Moons to make it to the next level. To get most of them he's going to have to complete challenging quests. Get started lending a helping hand to the people of the city and the moons will start rolling in.

The Mayor of the city needs help restoring the power back to the city. Even though Bowser has already been there and talked about his wedding, now it is time for the mayor to think about the citizens that are living there. Can Mario help her out?

Ride down the spark pylon to the outskirts of the city. Make sure to swat all the larvae that you come into contact with using Cappy before they hatch, or they might cause further problems later on. Be careful to sidestep the larvae and try not to get in their way; they have amazing tempers and they literally blow up when someone stands before them.

Better yet, grab a scooter and you can run right over those larvae as you pass them. Plus, you can get around the outskirts a bit easier and with more style when you're on one of the scooters.

Since one of Bowser's advertisements is in the pathway you need to travel down, you'll have to take the other path and drive past the Sherms to the City Hall. Go into the construction site from there. Capture a Sherm to use on this level and drive to the nearest suspended beam. Here you'll want to travel up to the ? block and use Cappy to strike it.

Go through the construction site, where you'll locate another Power Moon. Then you can skirt around to the front of City Hall.

From here, you can capture one of the Sherms that's blocking the doorway and use it to blast the other Sherms out of the way. Just make sure to fire constantly, because you don't want them to catch you! Be careful to wipe out any larvae heading your way with the Sherm as well.

Now climb up to the first rooftop. Use a series of wall jumps or the spark pylon to get across to the heliport. Look above the swaying beam andgrab the Power Moon that is resting there. Now enter into the City Hall from the door in the adjacent building to where you are.

Run across the crumbling areas, down to where the striped poles are. Jump down here, taking care to skip the next landing to go even further. Leap from pole to pole across from you to get to the treasure chest that's waiting on the other side.

Finally, use the Spark Pylon to get to the rooftop where you're going to meet the boss of this level, a mechanical beast with quite the temper.

Mechawiggler is the beast that so many are afraid of, but it's your duty as Mario to battle him. Use a Sherm to blast through this beast with all your might. He is going to be spitting and spewing at you, so blast him while moving around to dodge the attacks. You can't stop for anything or you'll take serious damage almost immediately. Use the Sherm to blast in the areas where it seems like he is folded into himself. This will eliminate more than just one section of his body, allowing you to win faster.

Once he goes dark, you can stop blasting but then he will turn gold after a bit. He's invincible now, but don't worry, you won't have to battle him any longer. He'll disappear through a portal and you'll be brought down to a platform where you can move on with your journey.

HELPING THE CITY GET A FRESH START

Since the destruction of the Mechawiggler, the city has changed including the Warp Flags and the rain that wouldn't stop before. Come morning, the city is back to itself and Bowsers ads are all removed from the city limits.

Go to City Hall to find Mayor Pauline and help her find four musicians that can play in the festival that she is putting together. The first one is right outside of the City Hall. He is a drummer. Once you talk with him, you're presented with a Power Moon. The next musician can be found in the Mayor Pauline Commemorative Park, he is a bassist. Use the Spark Pylon to get here as fast as possible.

Use the poles on the side of the building outside the Cafe to flick Mario up to the rooftop. Talk with the trumpeter that is waiting on the top of the room to get another Power Moon. The last musician can be found on Main Street in the corner of the park. He is a guitarist that is also going to provide a Power Moon.

TIME TO POWER UP THE STATION

In order to get the most from the festival, Mayor Pauline needs a bit more help from Mario. This time, he has to lift open the manhole and go into the sewers of the city. The manhole is located in front of the cafe.

This is the underground power plant. To get things started you'll want to go down the walkway and into the second pipe. Spin each of the platforms to help you get from one side to the next. Do this by throwing Cappy to get the platform spinning, a bonus to this technique is that it also helps to keep the poison away from you. With the platforms in motion it's up to you to jump from one to the next to get around. At the top ledge of this platform, there is a Power Moon hidden right above it.

Mayor Pauline will meet you down by this platform before you can reach the Power Moon. It's here that you'll have to fight a poison plant. Defeat the Poison plant to stop the poison from being sent everywhere and earn another Power Moon in the process. Now all you have to do is ground pound the red button on the floor to get the festival started!

PUTTING ON A TRUE FESTIVAL

The glorious festival has begun, and you're busy celebrating and having a good time, but of course there's another challenge for you to get through. During the big event you're taken up on stage with the band and a new mural is erected on the side of one of the buildings that looks just like Mario himself. This is for all your help with the city and how thankful they are.

You will have to go through an 8-bit level and it can take some time to master. Just keep your patience and go through the level as smoothly as you can. Avoid any of the barrels and fire pits that come into play, while also hitting the blocks for coins. This is from back in the classic Mario days, so it is a bit of an enjoyment level before moving onto the next kingdom.

Once you make it through the 8-bit level, you are awarded with another Power Moon. Just like the 80's classic. Enjoy this complex level, it adds another element of fun to the game and creates some challenges that you aren't likely to encounter during other areas of the game.

COLLECT MORE POWER MOONS

Now all Mario has to do is collect enough Power Moons to power up the aircraft and fly out of there. With so many of them hiding around this city, a little searching is all it takes to build up the collection high enough.

Check out each of the following locations when moving through the city. Rooftop flower pots, RC car racing grounds and in the park where you found the guitarist. You're not able to leave until you have collected enough to repair the Odyssey and to keep flying to the next levels.

- The area contains 100 regional coins that are hidden as you go along the various quests. while moving about you need to look up on the rooftops and balconies, as you drive the scooter. There are many nooks and crannies, but most of the regional coins for the area are out in the open.
- The area also contains a high number of Power Moons to collect, with 81 total in the area. You already know how to come across some of them, but make sure to hop on the buildings, in the trash and to question Captain Toad and to search in the cafe.

SHIVERA

This is the land of ice and snow and it is where Cappy and Mario land next. It is a land where shivering is a common occurrence, but the locals are friendly and warm. The area is simple to get through and most of the quests are quite short, which is good for us because we're already getting chilly!

Just like the previous kingdoms, Mario has quests he must fulfill to get the Power Moons to get the Odyssey up and running. In order to do this though, he's going to have to battle through each of the quests.

On top of the snowy plateau, you will find a mound of snow. Throw Cappy at it to knock off the snow and then dive down into the well below.

GOING THROUGH FOUR MAIN ROOMS

Bowser has taken off with a cake and now Mario has to chase after him in order to get it back. He is going to have to go through four different rooms along in his journey. This was a great gift planned for the after-the-race festivities , so now Mario has to catch up to him to try and get it.

Wander through the the halls once you land in the city below through the well. You will come across four different rooms with objectives in each one.

THE ICICLE CAVERN

This is a slippery area and it's easy to slide right off to your doom. That's why you need to make heavy use of Goombas while traveling here. They offer more traction, while also working to break down the icicles. If you notice a dangling shadow above you, use the Goomba to gently coax it down and make sure it does not fall on Mario!

When you have at least four Goombas you can open up a wall of ice and uncover Power Moons that are hidden behind it. Once you collect the two Moons here, you can bound up the stairs, being careful to dodge the icicles and slippery terrain. At the top, you will find even more Goombas that you can use along the way.

In the corner of the top room, you'll notice a stack of crystals in one of the corners. Use a Goomba to knock this stack apart and then break it to make way for the Power Moon to come out, but also for the exit pipe to show up.

HOLLOW CREVICE

Head to the top right spoke next. This is a room with square water pools filled up. There are five Power Moons hidden in this level and you have to run around and collect them all. Oh! There are also going to be BiteFrosts and of course, monsters that jump up at you so battle your way through the room while making sure they don't get you. Try to stay out of the water, since there aren't any hidden shards to find in this area.

Jump to the top, collect the last Power Moon and use the pipe to get out of there once they have all been collected.

SNOWY MOUNTAIN

The left spoke is where the next little room is located. Use the hat trampolines to get in there and to the tops of the room to collect the coins and other goodies that have been left behind. There is a gap in the wall, throw Cappy to remove the snow that's build up here and then enter the crevice. Follow the hallway until you reach the end, where you will find another Power Moon. Go around the corner where you're going to find another boss to battle.

RANGO THE BOSS

Rango is an intense boss that makes use of blazed buzz saw hats to try and take you out. This villain is going to do anything possible to keep you from succeeding in your quest, allowing Bowser to escape once and for all. Break the rocks in the floor during the battle to unearth hearts, just make sure to keep your footing, as it can become quite slippery.

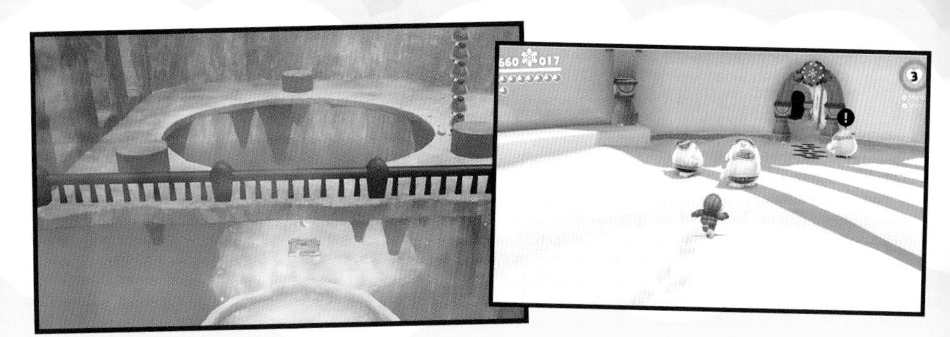

Block the hat throws that Rango makes with Cappy and by doing so you'll create a set of trampolines that you can use against Rango himself. All those flipped hats can be used to jump up on Rangos head. Hop up there and you'll do damage to the boss. Rango will go a little crazy after getting hit and then go back to throwing. You have to do the same moves and jump on his head again to finish him off. He will walk away after this and you will receive another Power Moon.

WIND CHILL CAVERN

This is a frosty place. Travel down through the bottom left spoke. The one serious danger present in Wind Chill Cavern is violet goo, so avoid it as much as possible. It can mean death if you land in it. Make it through this room and you'll start racing in the Icy Kingdom once again.

The entire room is moving and Mario must jump from Ty-Foo to Ty-Foo without losing his footing. The moment you lose your footing, you'll end up in the goo, which means death and we don't want that. You want to make sure that you keep in mind that these gusts will knock you down, so be quick but keep your footing.

Travel to the archway where the Power Moon is hidden and grab it before descending back down to the moving platforms. Take care of the Spinies on the lower platform and then reveal another hidden Power Moon.

BE PART OF THE RACE

To start up the race, head down the tube into the Snowline Circuit. There is a waiting room off to the right. Enter there and sit and wait for the next race to begin.

When you're ready to get in the race, you will be against seven others. Over the length of the course you'll be challenged by four wide 90 degree turns, so tread with caution. There are many tricks and traps that you'll encounter while going through the course so pay close attention and keep your eye on the road ahead. When you first try to get into the race the locals aren't willing to let him join because he's small and not well-suited to the environment. Cappy can help you be part of the action, though.

Shiverian Elder
Our Frost-Frosted Cake was stolen,
so the prize will be

Since Cappy is able to capture the things in front of him, you just have to throw Cappy out to the driver and you can capture it to use in the race. You can use all their driving abilities, which helps maintain control of the car — this race is for the locals, after all.

You must be mindful of the traction as you round the corners. Keep a close eye on your opponents and make sure to give it some gas. To enhance your speed during the race, bound whenever you have a large amount of straight space ahead of you. Just be careful to avoid bounding with a corner coming up because you can't turn until after. The winner gets a Power Moon at the end.

- A Cheep Cheep can help you stay alive while you swim in the water for both warmth and oxygen. Capture one for longer periods of time in the icy waters.
- There are 50 regional coins to find hidden throughout the kingdom. Some of the places to check for them include bottomless looking pits, high up in the clouds and in the waiting room in Snowline Circuit where you waited to start the race.
- There are also 55 Power Moons to find as you go along. You get some for defeating the bosses that you come across, but you can also get them in random areas such as in the shining snow, at the entrance of the town, swimming in the freezing water and slipping behind the ice walls.

SEASIDE KINGDOM

BUBBLAINE

Welcome to the wonderful kingdom of Bubblaine, where anything is possible and where water rules the world around the inhabitants. Mario must go through this level in order to get closer to Princess Peach. It's up to you to make sure he completes the quests and gets the right amount of Power Moons to keep moving forward, so pay attention.

MARIO'S QUESTS FOR THE SEASIDE KINGDOM

Just like the other kingdoms before, Mario must complete quests and obtain the right amount of Power Moons in order to move onto the next level. You can expect a real challenge while working through this water Kingdom.

WHERE DID THE SPARKLE WATER GO?

Upon arrival, Mario will speak with a snail-like creature that calls this kingdom his home. He shows Mario the fountain used to fill up the area with bubbly-like sparkle water but currently, the glass is half empty and they need help finding out why and how to fix it. Mario realizes the pipes are clogged up, so he must go around to all four and unclog them.

STONE PILLAR

The stone pillar is the first seal that Mario has to unclog. The switch that will unclog this area is right offshore, but on a tall piece of land. Use a Gushen to propel Mario up to the top of the land so he can ground pound the switch and unclog the seal. Once this is completed, you'll receive a Power Moon for your efforts.

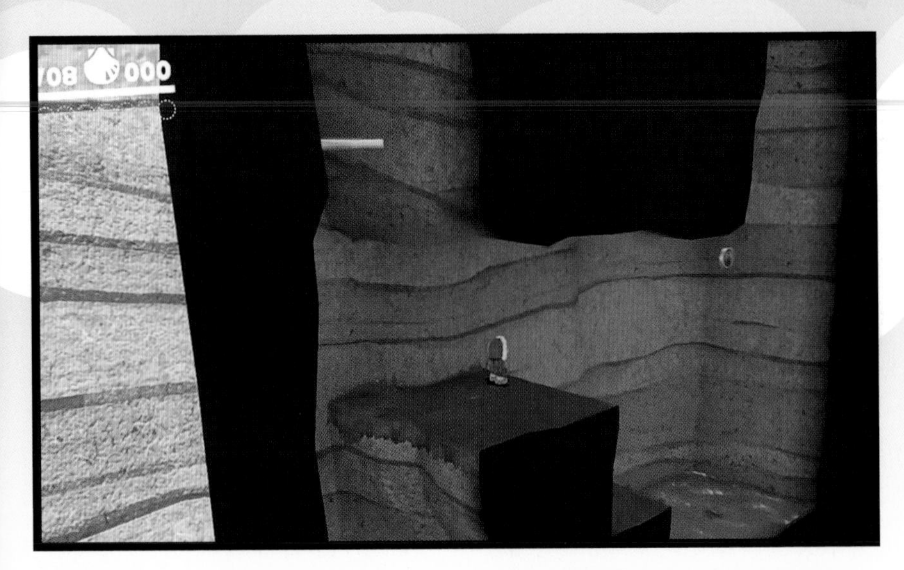

LIGHTHOUSE

The switch to unclog this seal is resting atop the lighthouse but you have to take an indirect route to get there. Go to the northern area of land and find a well. Once you locate the well, take a deep breathe a jump in! This leads straight to the lighthouse.

At the bottom of the well you'll reach an underground tunnel underneath the lighthouse. Use a Cheep Cheep to get through this section. You'll need all the air you can get to make it through the hallways, be sure to keep an eye out for the Maw Rays lurking around corners and in cracks while exploring. These can actually kill Mario if they end up hitting him, so you will want to swim clean and fast through the tunnels as the Cheep Cheep.

Once the screen starts to shake, a giant Maw Ray will jump out and snap at Mario. Keep swimming and dodging the attacks that will come throughout the hallway. Be sure to collect all of the regional coins as you go. At the end, the screen will shake again, just keep to the middle of the screen, because many MawRays are going to attack. Just keep swimming.

Cross over the tunnel and then you have made it to the top of the lighthouse. You want to ground pound the switch and once this is activated you will receive another Power Moon.

HOT SPRING

On your way to Hot Spring Island make sure you check out Sand Bar Island. Look under the bar to find a hidden Moon that has been purposely placed there. You'll need to ground pound to unearth it. While here, go through the small tunnel holding your breath along the way. About halfway you will find a Power Moon, which restores your oxygen and health before reaching the end of the tunnel.

Once you get there, the hot springs are going

to be covered in molten lava. Capture a Gushen and use it to spray water over the lava to cool it down, flying back and forth over it. Once you're up in the air, you can shake the controller to use a 360 water spin action to put out the lava.

After the lava is under control, hit the warp flag and then dive into the pool below. You will find a Power Moon hidden there, along with the next switch that works to unclog the seal.

ABOVE THE CANYON

The seal heading to the Sparkle Water Fountain is the last one that needs to be broken. Touch the warp pole at the bottom of the canyon, because this is a checkpoint. Capture a Goomba and then start your trek up the side of the canyon walls. Just make sure to watch for the angry Goombette that might be waiting there. If you rendezvous with the fairest Goomba there, you can collect another Power Moon.

Ditch the Goomba and run up the side of the canyon. Just make sure to jump over and dodge any shells that come tumbling down along the way. Once you get to the top of the canyon, there will be three boxes. You want to break them open using Cappy and then collect the Power Moon. Once you do this, the switch for the last seal will come out. Ground pound this to unclog the seal.

Now the octopus that thinks he's the master of the kingdom has been knocked off his perch and he's angry and seaking revenge!

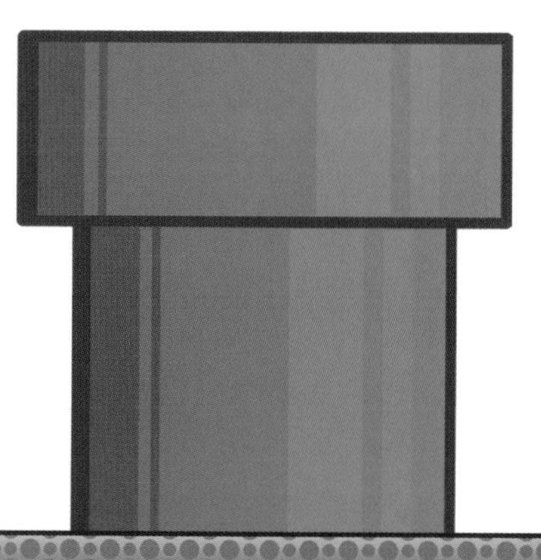

BRIGADIER MOLLOSQUE-LANCEUR III, DAUPHIN OF BUBBLAINE

When he arises, you will notice that he's covered in lava, your first task is to cool him down as much as you can. Capture another Gushen and use the spray feature to cover the octopus in water. Do your best to get him in the face. Start off spraying close to the octopus and then move away after you start your attack for the best possible shot.

As a Gushen, he will have a hard time chucking shells at Mario, so keeping away from him and flying over his head is a good idea. As long as you fight him properly, the Octopus boss is going to get furious, and the moment he does he will begin throwing drill bit pieces towards you. Dodge them while continuing to spray at him. Of course, you're going to want to ground pound him a few times.

Once you get his health most of the way down, set your aim to the top of his head and use a super ground pound to knock him out. You will have to continue to do this until he runs away, usually all it takes is around three times. You receive a Power Moon once he is defeated.

- 100 purple regional coins can be found throughout the region. Check in the high places, as well as the tunnels hidden throughout the lands underwater.
- 71 Power Moons can be found throughout the kingdom, but Mario only needs 10 to keep flying. Some of the areas that these can be found include nesting spots, the back of the canyon, in the waves and in the glass palace treasure chest.

LUNCHEON KINGDOM

MOUNT VOLBONO

Everything is cooking hot with a volcano, so you can expect this kingdom to be none other than the hottest. Volcanic eruptions are happening all the time here, so keep a close eye on when and where they are occurring, so you're prepared for any eruptions that might come close to you. Anything can happen!

WHAT IS ON MARIO'S QUEST LIST

Luncheon Kingdom is jam packed with tough quests, but don't be worried, your efforts won't go unnoticed! You'll be rewarded with not only great food and good times, but also Power Moons which you need to keep your journey running smoothly. You can see Bowser's ship flying in circles overhead, which is just more motivation to keep moving because you're getting dangerously close to the villain once and for all.

REMOVING UNWANTED VISITORS

The townspeople are very nice and welcoming, but when someone visits that they do not want, they want to have him removed. It is up to Mario to find these unwanted guests and make sure that they leave the nice people alone.

Go to the Old Town to do some exploring. Capture a Goomba and then put all of the specimens in a stack. Head for the giant piece of corn and dodge all the dangers that are lurking in the way. This looks like a giant corn cob, bigger than little Mario and it should be towards the corner of the room.

Jump up on the giant corn and walk towards the stack of Goombas that you've created. You can use this corn as a rolling platform while going over lava. Bring the captured Goomba stack to the Goombette by grabbing them and rolling over the lava with the corn. Once you do so, you're gifted with another Power Moon.

Go to the little pathway made of acid-water. Capture a Lava Bubble and swim through the pathway to get out at the other side.

BOSS SPEWART HAS BEEN AWAITING YOU

Spewart is known to spit out poison, so it is up to you to stay away from the spurting that he does. You don't want to be caught in it when it is being spit out and you don't want to step in it, so make sure to dodge and weave throughout this fight.

You will make Spewart mad, but use Cappy to knock the hat off his head. Without it, he is useless and will begin to jump around. After his hat has been knocked off, you have to move quick and bounce on top of his head. Once you do this, you'll be well on your way to winning the fight, but you'll have to repeat your steps a few times for real success.

Once you finally win the fight you get another Power Moon to add to your collection, so keep up the good work and the Odyssey will be flying around in no time!

THOSE CHEESE ROCKS LOOK TASTY, DON'T THEY?

Mario has to climb higher in the mountains, but he has to go down to the town for a bit. The giant stew pot that once held the delicious stew is now empty and much too hot to touch. Bowser has come and taken the food to claim as his own. Mario has to help the town get their stew back, while also saving the peppered meat that is now in peril.

Go through the narrow alleyway right by Crazy Cap's building and walk down it. You will come to a large pile of crates laying there. Break through the crates to get some goodies, including another Power Moon.

Notice the long pillars throughout the town. These are great for power jumping to and fro. There's a special technique you need to use to get to the top of the pillars though. Triple jump to get to the proper height for the pillars, and once you're up there you'll find a Power Moon just waiting for you to come and grab it.

Next, new ingredients must be found and then added to the pot to get the stew cooking. This next step helps the pizza owner throw in some delicious ingredients to get it going. Just make sure to not touch the pot — it is still too hot!

Look for three golden turnips hidden throughout Luncheon Kingdom. Add all three to the pot and each of them will give a Power Moon reward. One of the turnips is hiding right next to Crazy Cap's Shop. Throw a hat at the sprout to pick it out of the ground. Pick up the turnip and then take a running leap to throw it up and into the pot.

Next, go to the bubbling lava and capture Lava Bubbles to throw into the pot. They will become the delicious tomatoes for the stew. Be careful that you do not touch the side of the pot, as this is very hot! Once you throw one in, collect your Power Moon reward!

THE BIG POT WELCOMES YOU

As the townspeople continue to collect ingredients to add to the pot to make another stew, you have to be prepared to dive right in when they need you to.

Go past the Meat Plateau checkpoint and into the narrow path. You are going to pass a decent amount of Fire Bros and Magmatoes. Follow the path, go over the skinny bridge over the open air until you get to a wall that has a Volbonan stuck in it. Release this townsperson and go further up the wall to release another.

Continue to move up the wall and find not only a checkpoint, but also a giant piece of spiced meat that is ready for the pot! You'll need to crack through that hard salty shell in order to get the meat free. Before you jump off the wall though, you can look over and notice that there is a Power Moon to your side.

A giant bird is going to swoop down, so grab the Moon, grab the meat and then jump down the wall. Remember, Mario doesn't take fall damage, so you do not have to worry about his health when you make it to the bottom of the ledge.

CASCADING MAGMA IS THE NEXT STEP

All of this ruckus has caused a commotion through the entire kingdom. Now there is a bird flying around the pot, the meat is free from the clutches of the salt and the pot is bubbling and boiling. A shift in the world has caused another piece of land to show itself. It's crowded by lava pathways.

You will have to explore this new land, but in order to do so, you have to wrap around the rock walls all the way around. You don't want to find yourself falling into any of the lava as you go, so keep a firm hold as you shimmy.

Go to the Volcano Cave Entrance flag, here you'll enter into the volcano. You will have to go up in the 8-bit playing field since there is such a wide gap between the entrance and where you stand.

Now all you have to do is roll the corn cob across the lava floors and jump to collect the regional coins in this area. Swerve to the left and right to collect more. Go up the pathway and then enter into the volcano's entrance.

The moment you walk in, you'll fall into the geyers. Once you do look to your side and you'll notice a sheer curtain covering a room to the side of you. This is where another Power Moon is hidden. Run into the room and grab it before continuing on.

Go into the alcove and use a Lava Bubble to swim over to where there are three lanterns. Use the bubble to light them up, revealing the next Power Moon that's hidden within the depths of this volcanic cave.

Going around this way allows for rear access to the mountain.

SHOWDOWN WITH A COCKATIEL

Next up is the showdown that you have been waiting for. This large bird boss has been following you all around the kingdom since you took that last piece of salted meat. Make sure you enter into this section with care, using the walls around you to leap from, while making sure not to touch the plants that stick out from the sides.

While going down the pathway, use the side stones that you come to to avoid the rolling veggies, while also helping you get to the end of the pathway quicker. Trying to jump over them might be tricky, as they can be quite large.

Once you get to the end, you must keep going. The only way to go is through a Lava Bubble that you capture and then swim across to the next platform.

Cookatiel will meet you at the end of the platform and that's when the fight begins. Watch out for the spikes that he spits from his mouth and down into the stew. Always keep your eyes on him, since anything can happen when you drop your attention for any period of time. The bird will spew out liquid everywhere. This is poison, so avoid it at all costs.

All you have to do is watch where he is spewing, grab a Lava Bubble and jump on his head. Once you do this, you can keep jumping until he gives in and flies away.

- There are 100 regional coins throughout the kingdom. Make sure to check out all the high places, as well as those that go through the bubbling lava.
- 68 Power Moons are floating around the area. Some you have to earn, some you can purchase and some you can find hidden in certain places such as on top of taller mountains, in the cheese rocks and at Captain Toad.

RUINED KINGDOM

CRUMBLEDEN

You're one step closer to the real deal and actually going up against Bowser. With all of the kingdoms that you have left behind, it's no wonder you're running out of steam. Now it is time challenge yourself a bit more then fly straight ahead, because what awaits you after this is going to be a lot of work. Are you ready to accept the challenge?

MARIO'S PLANS FOR THE AREA

Just like all the other Kingdoms, it's up to Mario to take on the quests, track down the regional coins and gather up all the Power Moons in this kingdom as well.

THE LORD OF LIGHTNING CALLS TO MARIO

You will have to battle the Lord of Lightning in order to get out of this kingdom and go onto the next.

Go to the swords in the ground and use Cappy to pull each of them up out of the earth below. Each of them is going to reveal coins, while the end one is going to give a Spark Pylon. Ride the pylon to wherever it leads — there is nowhere else to go, is there?

The Pylon brings you to the second tallest tower that you see off in the distance earlier on. While up here in this intimidating location you'll naturally run into one of Bowser's greatest weaopns — the Ruined Dragon.

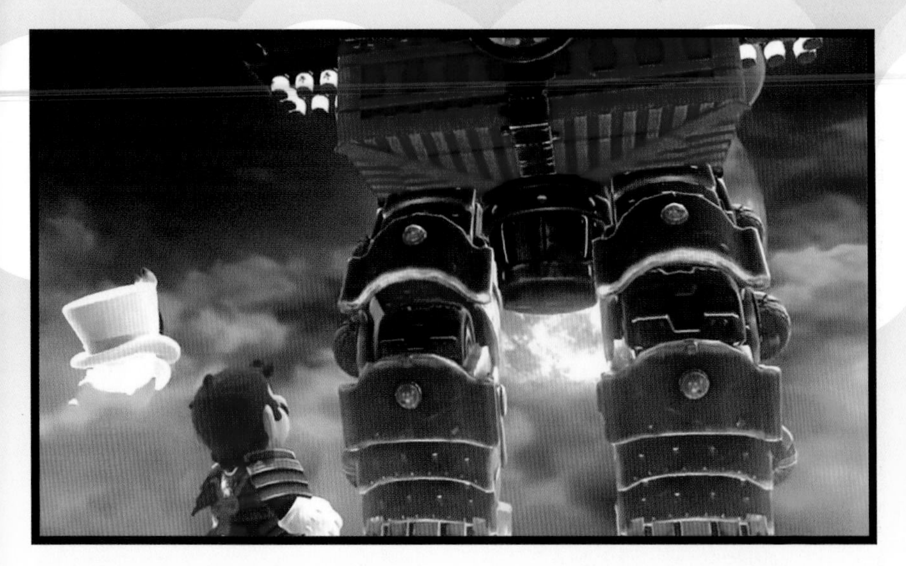

The dragon is puzzled at first when he notices Mario at the edge of his basin. Make sure to keep your distance, because he's not puzzled for very long and then he breathes out lightning. Dodge the lightning when you can, but the best way to stay out of the way is to keep your distance.

Once he goes through the shots and then the rings, you will notice he sends jolting waves of electricity through the ground. Mario must use his jump rope practice here and jump over the electricity as it comes to him. Once this ends however, Mario must be ready to jump on the dragon's face.

Use Cappy to remove the swords that are lodged in the top of the dragon's head. Once removed you can remove the cap that is controlling him. With the swords removed, the crown cracks and becomes vulnerable. This leaves Mario open for a ground pound.

Throughout this entire fight you'll be dodging the Burrbos that come popping up. You only have a limited time to remove the swords and then ground pound him. You need to be quick, so step lively and get the job done.

If you need life during this battle, check the outside ring of the arena for glowing spots. These are where you you'll find some hidden hearts to revitalize you as needed.

You'll must ground pound the dragon's head three times in order to defeat him. You will get a Power Moon with ever pound that you make on his head, which is enough to get you the heck out of there!

- Ruined Kingdom does not hold any regional coins, so you don't have to keep an eye out for these while visiting this deserted kingdom.
- There are 10 Power Moons in total that can be collected here, but not all of them can be found upon the first visit. You must come back to collect the rest.

BOWSER'S KINGDOM

BOWSER'S CASTLE

By now, you've probably realized you're going to have to visit Bowser's castle in order to find Princess Peach. You should rejoice knowing that you made it this far in the Odyssey. With such a long journey, you'd think that it would stop here — but it doesn't. Make sure to collect more Power Moons and keep on moving along after the quests that await you here.

JOURNEY THROUGH...... TO BOWSER YOU GO......

Go past the advance gate, check out the Goomba guards on patrol and make a stack with them by capturing them one by one. Head to the right, then follow the curl around the hallway. This leads to a special button. You must have a stack of 10 Goombas in order to get it to work. Luckily for you, you should already have them all gathered up at this point.

Hop onto the stack to get the Power Moon that's just above you on the ledge. Then grab the regional and gold coinswaiting for you. Grab the Spark Pylon that shows up after you do this.

You will land in a floating courtyard. Make sure to grab the checkpoint here, in case something happens to you during the rest of your trip. Capture a Pokios and then flick yourself up to the roof to grab the Power Moon. Once you have itclimb back down. Keep in mind, you're getting further into the castle now, so the guards are going to become much more serious.

Use the Spark Pylon to go to the third courtyard just to the side of the one you're in. Go to the next battlement using the Spark Pylon, grab the Warp Flag and then head up the stairs in front of you. Just make sure to avoid the Spinies while doing all this!

The Staircase Ogre will be to your right as you go up the stairs resting on a platform. These ogres will try to stamp on Mario every time he is around. Dodge the stamping and take note of the staircase that comes down each time the ogre stomps. You need to ground pound him, take your Power Moon and then double jump to grab the ladder and go right up it.

BOWSER RAMPS UP HIS DEFENSES

Bowser knows that Mario is getting closer, and he will do all he can to get rid of him. In this next level, the bombs will rain down upon you, so prepare for the worst.

You will end up in the second courtyard, where you'll notice many cannonball bombs released by Turrets falling down around you. Pokios will start coming around when this happens, but by capturing one, you can actually deflect the hit of the ball. They can turn the bombs around and shoot them back at the sender.

The first turret has a broken shard of Power Moon that must be put together in order to stop the madness. It was made this way so that intruders could not just come in and stop the destruction from happening. To gather these pieces, you just have to look in each of the following places:

- Under the first turret
- Hovering in front of the wall
- Over the fire pit
- Hidden in one of the bomb boxes between two of the turrets
- Tucked up on a ledge towards the back of the structure

Once the Power Moon is put together, you can open up the doors to the gate that reveals a Spark Pylon for Mario to ride down to the next level.

TIME FOR ANOTHER BATTLE

You're going to have to take on two of the bosses again when you come to the next room. Make sure to rest and relax before this fight, so you can go through both and come out the winner. Stop by the shop or relax by the comfortable woods to prepare.

Hariet is the first boss you're going to come against. You have already fought her before, so you should be somewhat familiar with what's to come. Go through the two golden Bowser statues to get to her. She'll throw her pigtail bombs right at you as soon as she hops from the ship above, so be prepared.

You will want to deflect and dodge the bombs as much as you can but it's not an easy task. She's relentless and is going to keep throwing them until you make her stop. Use a ground pound to jump on her head. She'll throw a fit when you do, but keep fighting and use Cappy to remove the hat from her head so you can beat her once and for all.

Repeat the cycle a few times in order to defeat her. When you do, another boss is standing there ready to take you on.

Topper is the next boss you're going to meet in this battle arena. You just have to step to the right of the platform to have him come out and start the next fight.

Always stay your distance from Topper because his Top Hat does damage in a short radius around him. His attacks often come without warning, but you'll be safe as long as you maintain a decent range from the boss.

Use Cappy to knock the stack of hats off his head. Keep up your attack until all of the hats are off. This is the only to get him open in order for Mario to beat him. Be ready with a ground pound assault the moment his head is free from his many hats. Just be mindful of the top hats that are going to try to stop you. Jump on them, dodge them and use Cappy to knock them out of the way.

Once you beat both of the bosses, you can easily grab the Power Moon and head to the next quest. You have to find Bowser!

BOWSER'S CASTLE, AT LAST!

Once you're done with those battles, you will be able to see Bowser's Castle straight ahead as you walk out of the gates. Grab the checkpoint in this area as you walk through and then head on to the castle. Rely on your binoculars to see what is happening up ahead of you and travel with care to avoid most of the danger.

Grab a Pokio and use it to climb the sides of the walls that extend to the outside of the platform. You'll quickly gain respect for the Pokio's climbing ability in this situation.

On the top of this wall, there will be skinny bridges that meet with one another. While crossing watch for the cannonballs coming from the turrets since they randomly shoot out, causing Mario to have to dodge on these skinny bridges. Whenever you're in danger and dodging isn't an option, your captured Pokio can send away the cannonballs using its beak.

Find the outer wall checkpoint as you follow the path. Grab the regional coins right in this area, as well.

This next task will take on a whole new level of game play. You're about to take on a two stage climbing wall that you have to get over with an ogre and mote down below it. Use the rotating disc that the ogre is wearing to move upward. Make sure to collect as many coins as you can on your way up.

Alternate on the conveyer belts that come and go to get across this level. The lighter colored sections of the wall can be pierced by the Pokio's beak but the other sections cannot. Move behind the spike strip on the left and you can gather some regional coins.

The last checkpoint that you're going to come across is behind a second run of obstacles stuck to a wall. Cross over the poison motes to the platform and then use the Spark Pylon to go to the roof of Bowser's Keep. However, it is not Bowser that Mario is up against. You get to meet with Koopa King instead.

Many of the members of Bowser's following have joined forces inside a major mechanical beast in order to take down Mario. It's able to stomp down on Mario, send out cannonballs and even spawn ground slithering snakes. Sometimes, the beast will use Pokios to help him, but this can come in favor since Mario can capture them and then use them to deflect the cannonballs.

Sending just one cannonball crashing into the beast can get the armor off of it. Crash them into the legs of the beast to have it fall down. You will have to knock the Robo beast down at least four times, since you need to be able to break the four globes that are sitting atop it's head.

Make sure to watch for a glowing light from the beast, as this signals that it is about to charge back and forth. When that happens make sure that Mario is well out of the way or it's all over with. This mechanical monster will become even more angry with each blow that he takes, causing him to change up his attack and become more difficult to defeat.

Ground pounding the globes, breaking all four and defeating this Robo beast brings on a Power Moon that you can collect at the end of the battle.

- 100 regional currency coins can be found throughout Bowser's Kingdom. You can check for them around the edges of structures and above doorways that you go into or pass.
- Bowser's Kingdom also has 62 Power Moons hidden within the walls of the fortress. You have to earn some of them through battles and quests, but you can also find them hidden throughout the castle in hidden corridors, under floors, in crates and in treasure chests hidden around the castle.

MOON KINGDOM

HONEYLUNE RIDGE

Just like a moon is what you can expect from this kingdom. It is dark and glowing and everything has a gray color to it. It is also one of those places that you don't know much about. You do know that it is your next stop to finding Bowser though, so you have to continue along.

THE MOON KINGDOM IS NOT WITHOUT QUESTS FOR MARIO...

Bowser is hoping for a moon wedding and when you arrive, you can see the Wedding Hall right off in the distance. Of course it's your number one priority to stop the wedding, since Princess Peach isn't interested in being stuck with Bowser forever. You'll be fighting through a series of challenges on the way to this goal though.

ZERO GRAVITY, BETTER JUMPS

Since this kingdom is not as large as the others, you want to do your best to play through the end of it on your own. Find the hidden regional coins, as well as the Power Moons to complete the mission here. Of course, keep in mind that any jumps you make will be much higher than normal since gravity is very low here.

Start your trip going down each of the pathways and be careful to grab the checkpoints as you go along. These are important in case you run across something particularly nasty that will take you out.

THOSE MOON CAVERNS ARE UNDERGROUND

Drop down below the platform where you'll get your gravity back. You will also be in an area that is hot and has lava, so keep that in mind. As soon as you can, capture one of the Parabones that are flying about. They're going to hwr the lava and the platforms ahead.

While questing you'll find cages with locked items inside. To open them up you just have to capture a Sherm and blast the cages apart and gather the items within. You need to open the Spark Pylon cage in order to advance to the next level, but grabbing the life-up heart is beneficial, too!

Ride the Spark Pylon and slap the big red button that awaits you at the end of the ride. Your platform will start to move and you will see Hammer Bros. Capture one of these since you will need to use their rain of hammers in order to break through the way ahead.

Ground pound the second red button thatyou get to and this will get the next platform moving to the next stop. Capture a Tropical Wiggler to use as you journey to the next area. You will want to use them to collect the coins you see along the way. Once you're at the end, you can ditch the wigglerand move on.

You will notice that Banzai Bill is demolishing the walls ahead and barreling down the bridge, right towards you! Use two cap throwsto capture him and then ride him over the lava and the platforms ahead.

Once you get into the room, ground pound the red button to get the platform moving to the next area. When you start moving, you can try to grab the regional coins that are there by reaching out or throwing your cap in their direction.

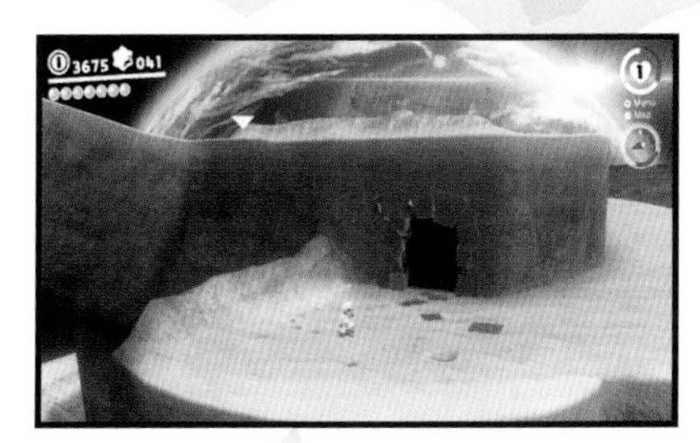

Keep your eyes open since the Moe-Eye's hidden bridge is where you're going to be crossing and when you get to the other side, prepare for a showdown with another one of the bosses that come to play. You want to run along the rocks and the bridges, capture Chuck and then hold onto him so that you can use his dash to get over the rocks and crevices that you come across in the road. These tiny gaps can cost you your life, so using the dash power helps you quickly move over them. Just make sure to watch out for any oncoming rocks.

Go up and almost all of the way out of the cavern, then jump onto the next Spark Pylon.

Using the Pylon brings you face to face with Madame Broode once again and she is just as angry as she was before. Just like you had to do before, you have to dodge her chains that she sends out, while also knocking her hats off her head with Cappy. Once the hat is off, ground pounding her can help you defeat her. Keep this momentum going. You'll have to go through the steps a few more times to win.

Of course, once you do, she is just going to run off back to the lunar's surface and take off on her spaceship!

TIME TO CRASH THE BIG WEDDING

At last! You have arrived in the right place, at the right time and you are dressed to impress! Make sure to grab the checkpoint before moving forward!

Head on up to the Wedding Hall where you're sure to find everyone ready for the day's festivities, or what they think are going to be festival-like! Once you go through the main entrance of the hall, go off to the right to crack open a rock and grab the life-up heart, since you may need it!

Enter the foyer of the Wedding Hall and then barge through the front doors of the room.

BOWSER IS NOT GOING TO GIVE UP

Bowser wants Princess Peach so when you go through those doors, he is not going to just give her up to you. He's going to put up the fight of his life to keep her by his side, and he has a few new tricks up his sleeve, too!

Just like the last fight, you can expect to find the series of hats that you've come to know. You'll also have a white hat as a target once again. To win the fight Mario will have to capture the white hat and then use it against Bowser while also dodging the other hats down on the ground.

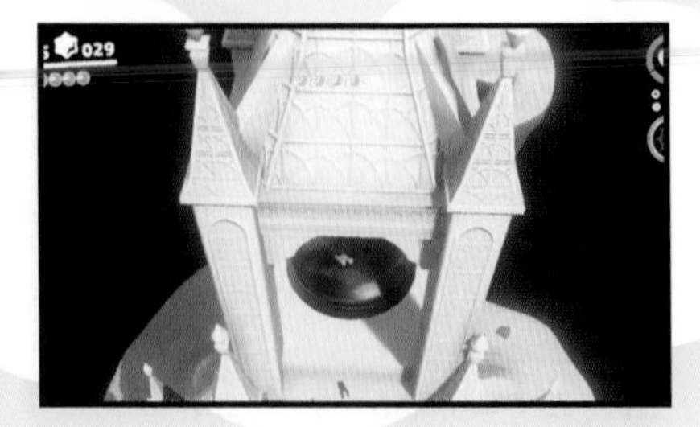

One thing that Bowser is going to do differently, though, is that he will send flames shooting out to cover the ground. Mario must be quick and jump over them before getting burned! Bowser then resorts to using boulders and cannonballs to try and stop Mario. However, Mario can break apart the boulders and the cannonballs can easily be jumped over or dodged. You just have to make sure that Mario is very agile and patient throughout this entire fight.

Watch out for Bowser's tail whip as he tries to take Mario out. Jumping over it is the most effective way to avoid the attack. Make Mario punch Bowser as much as possible in the face; this is the way to win. With each tail swipe, Mario can catch him on his way back around. With careful timing you can completely take control of the fight without taking much damage at all. Bowser will keep trying to tail whip Mario, but repeatedly punching him will bring him down before long.

AND THEN THE ESCAPE...

Winning three waves against Bowser can result in a victory for Mario. However, once the castle around them starts to shake and collapse, a route out of there is required. If no one is able to find a way out, this can mean that everyone might parish along with the building!

A breakable stone wall will appear and Mario will have to destroy it. Shake the controller to do so. This causes a fireball to be released into the wall, breaking it down, giving Mario an escape route. Just make sure to watch for boulders that will be falling down all around you.

Go to the main room from the escape tunnel. You will notice four pillars set up there. Dismantle each of the four pillars, but watch out as you do so, since you don't want anything from above falling down on you. Take them all out and then Cappy will let you know that the central block is now vulnerable.

Run to the center and focus all of your attacks on that one block.

- 50 Regional Coins can be found throughout the walls of this kingdom, so keep an eye out for them as you move along in your journey. Look under shallow bridges, in cannons and in the Wedding Hall.
- Only 38 Power Moons are hidden throughout this region, keep an eye out for them, with some of the areas not holding any at all. Check along the cliff face, in the rolling rocks all over the moon's surface, up in the rafters or even with the art.

MUSHROOM KINGDOM

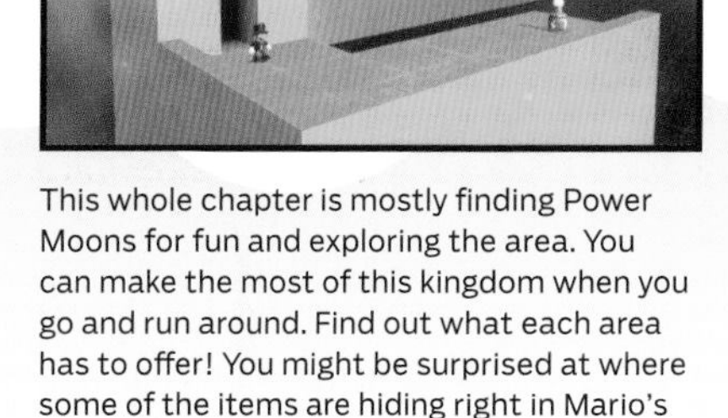

PEACH'S CASTLE

Peach's Castle is where she calls home, so it is no wonder it is a place you're going to go to next. With many things happening all at once, the people of the region want to know what happened to their Princess and how they're able to get her back! Don't worry though, Mario is here to save Princess Peach and the day!

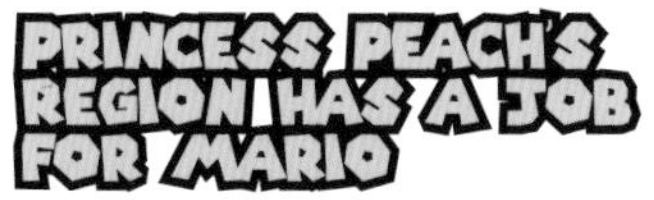

PRINCESS PEACH'S REGION HAS A JOB FOR MARIO

What kind of kingdom would this be if they did not ask Mario for a bit of his help? Mario still calls this kingdom his home and the townsfolk are just as happy as ever to see him and want to tell him of everything that has happened since he has been gone.

Check the castle to make sure Peach is still there and doing well and that she survived everything that has happened before. Of course, Peach and Tiara have already packed up by the time that you arrive, so you are going to have to come back again to see them.

This whole chapter is mostly finding Power Moons for fun and exploring the area. You can make the most of this kingdom when you go and run around. Find out what each area has to offer! You might be surprised at where some of the items are hiding right in Mario's own home town!

TIPS

- Find up to 100 regional coins hidden throughout the kingdom. Look up on the top of towers, in the tunnels below and those hovering over the drop offs.
- There are also 43 Power Moons hidden throughout the lands, so you want to check in many places. This is after all the only objective that this kingdom has for Mario to take on. Check out Peach's Castle, around the well and in the flower garden.

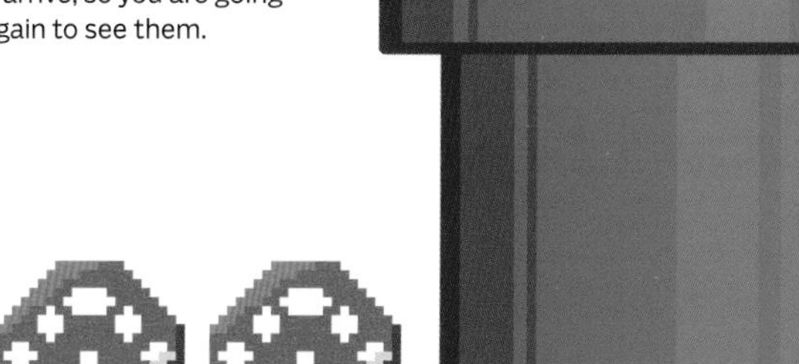

Head off to another kingdom?
Set Sail
Cancel

With so much happening in Mario Odyssey, there is so much more that can be said. We're sure you have found your own tips and tricks and created a strategy of your own to get through many of the areas. However, use our guide to help you get past some of the trickier areas that you come across.

You never know when you might be able to benefit from a helping hand along the way. Don't worry about failing a bit before you succeed, that's exactly how you'll make it through the tougher parts of the game.

Remember, just because you collected over 500 Power Moons does not mean you're done. There are literally hundreds more Power Moons waiting for you to collect them. You just have journey back to where you started and keep adding to the amount. Use the numbers provided above to count down the ones you have and the ones that are still left to find. That is the whole fun of the game — and beating Bowser!

Now it's time to get started on your journey, through the kingdoms and to allow Mario to have some jump time. He's come a long way, but he's always ready to rescue Princess Peach, and he'll have to work harder than ever before to succeed in Mario Odyssey.

If you think you have what it takes to succeed in the game, go out there and try to beat Bowser. Just make sure to stop every now and then to enjoy the worlds, to enjoy the townsfolk and enjoy all that the game has to offer, including the Cap Shops along the way that can provide some pretty sweet gear.

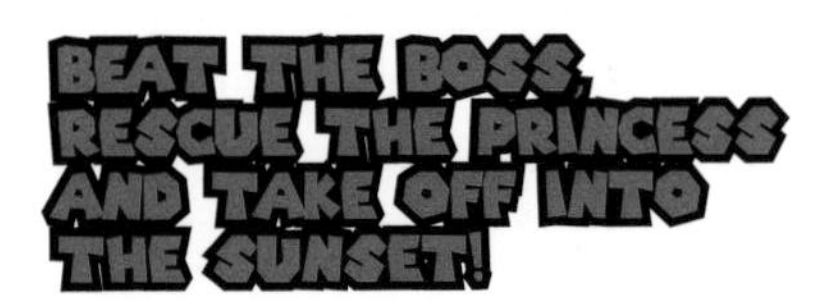
BEAT THE BOSS,
RESCUE THE PRINCESS
AND TAKE OFF INTO
THE SUNSET!

If you like Babymouse,
you'll love these other great books
by Jennifer L. Holm!

THE BOSTON JANE TRILOGY

EIGHTH GRADE IS MAKING ME SICK

MIDDLE SCHOOL IS WORSE THAN MEATLOAF

OUR ONLY MAY AMELIA

PENNY FROM HEAVEN

TURTLE IN PARADISE

THEY'RE REALLY GOOD! TRUST ME!

Read about my first graphic novel adventure in **Squish: Super Amoeba!**
yay.
I LOVE GRAPHIC NOVELS!! AND SLIME MOLD!!!
Oh, and by the way: It isn't pink.

WHAT'S WRONG WITH PINK?

Nothing.
See you soon!

I STILL THINK YOU LOOK LIKE A BLOB.
DON'T BE JEALOUS, BABYMOUSE.

Hi. My name is Squish. I'm an amoeba.
YOU LOOK LIKE A BLOB.

I'm not a blob. I'm a single-celled organism.

I live in a pond . . .

And have two best friends.

Psst!
Do you like
graphic novels?
Then turn
the page.

Step Two: With the right thumb and index, pick up the string on the left palm, between the hanging strings, and pull it out slightly (Fig. 3).

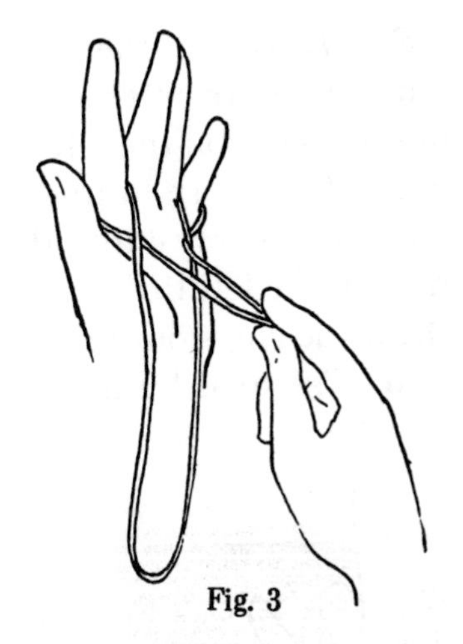

Fig. 3

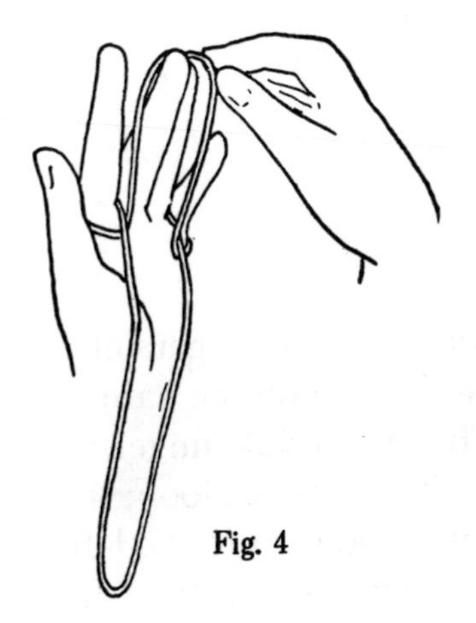

Fig. 4

Put it over the left middle and ring fingers (Fig. 4).

There is now a ring around the left index, a ring around the left little finger, and a loop hanging down on the palm (Fig. 5).

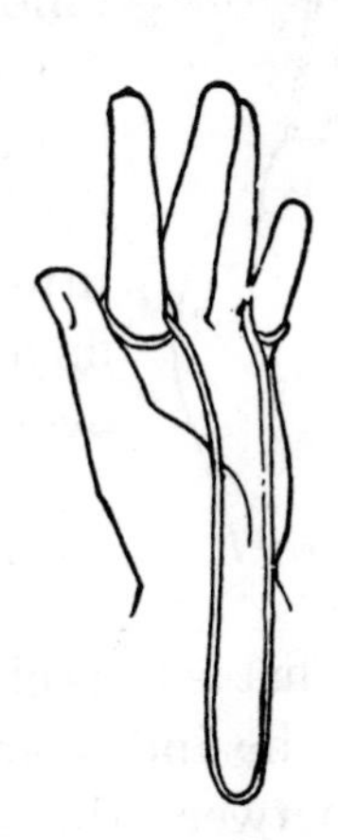

Fig. 5

Step Three: Put the right index finger from above into the ring on the left index. Put the right middle finger from above into the ring on the left little finger. Draw the rings out to the right (Fig. 6) as far as possible.

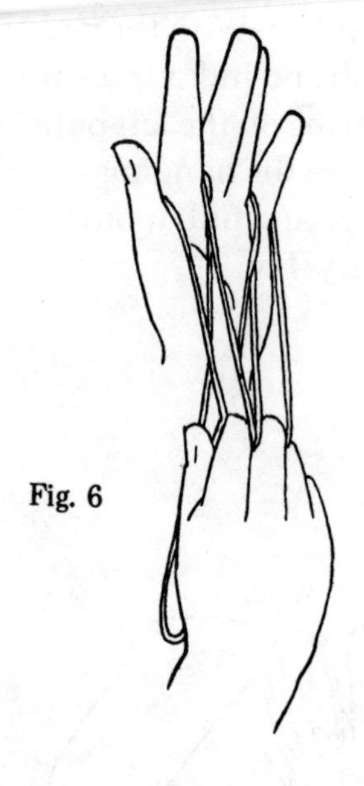

Fig. 6

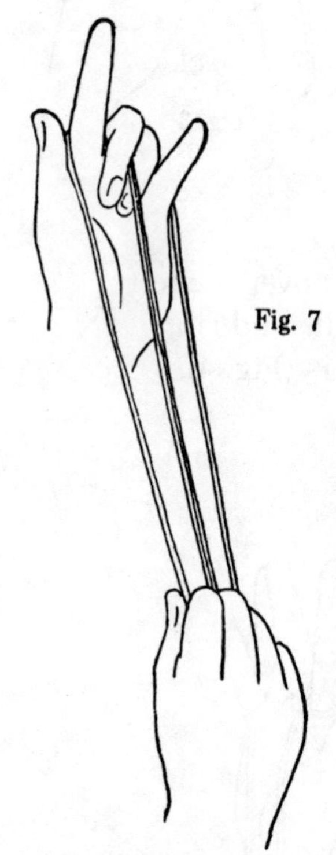

Fig. 7

Step Four: Bend the fingers of the left hand down on the palm as follows: The left middle finger down into the left index loop; the left ring finger down into the left little finger loop (Fig. 7); the left little finger over the left far little finger string, and the left index over the left near index string.

When the left fist is thus closed, you have a string coming out between the index and middle finger, two strings coming out between the middle and ring fingers, and a string coming out between the ring and little fingers.

Over the backs of the fingers, at their bases, there is a string around the index finger, a string around both the middle and ring fingers, and a string around the little finger (Fig. 8).

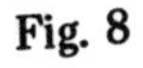
Fig. 8

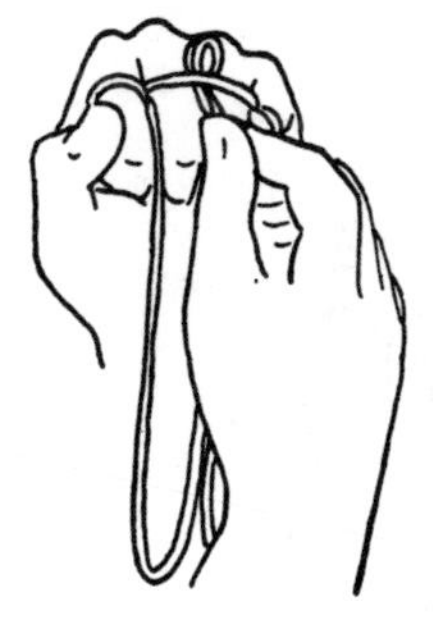
Fig. 9

Step Five: With the thumb and index of the right hand, pull up slightly the string on the backs of the left middle and ring fingers, and pass the four strings coming out between the fingers of the left fist through this loop to the back of the hand (Fig. 9).

Let the strings, pulled entirely through, hang down on the back of the left hand (Fig. 10).

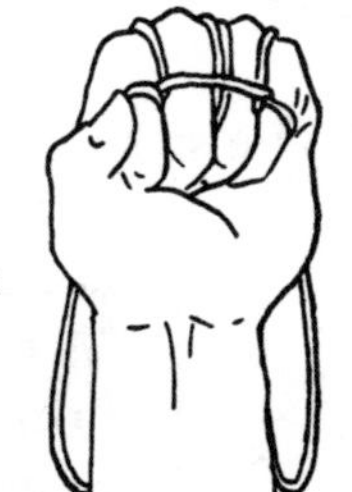
Fig. 10

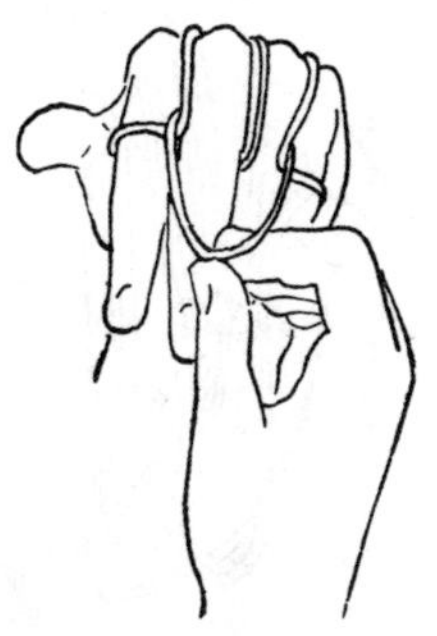
Fig. 11

Step Six: With the right thumb and index, pull this same loop crossing the backs of the left middle and ring fingers (through which you have just passed the four strings) over the knuckles of the middle and ring fingers (Fig. 11), and to the palm of the left hand.

Then draw it out to the right as far as possible, but carefully, and not too hard, at the same time unclenching the left fist. With some stretch of the imagination, you'll get the four candles tied together on the left hand (Fig. 12).

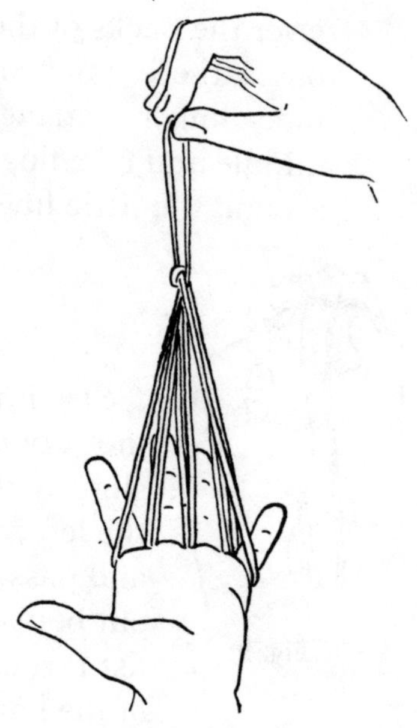

Fig. 12

The story of the candles is as follows:

> **"A man stole a pound of candles and, bringing them home, tied them together to hang on a peg."**

Step Seven: At this point, insert the left thumb, from below, into the loop held by the right thumb and index, and let the loop hang down on the left thumb (Fig. 13).

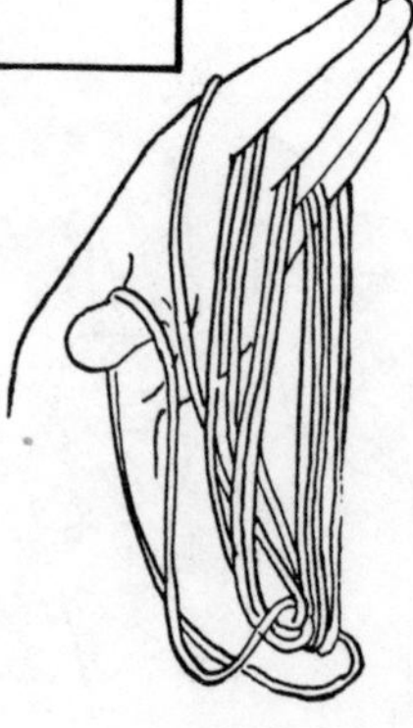

Fig. 13

"And being very tired, the man sat down on a chair and went to sleep."

Step Eight: Now, pointing the right index and middle fingers downward, over the back of the left hand held palm down with the fingers pointing to the right, take up, from the left side, on the ball of the right index, the loop on the back of the left middle finger; and take up on the ball of the right middle finger the loop on the back of the left ring finger (Fig. 14, seen from above).

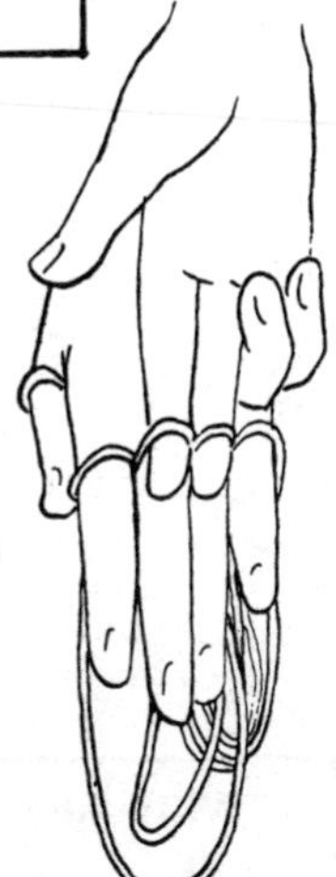

Fig. 14

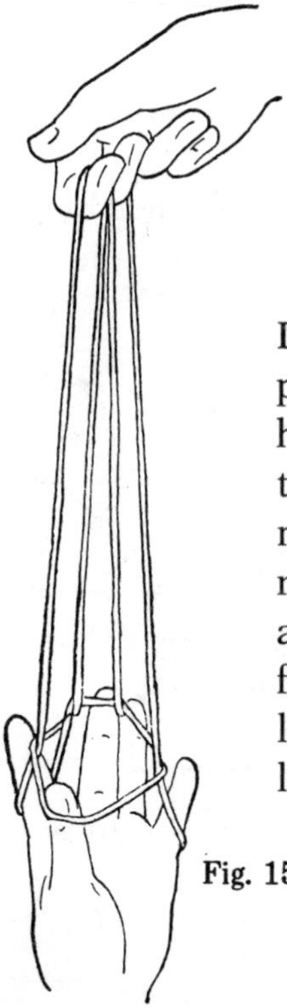

Draw the loops out as far as possible to the right. Turn the left hand with the palm upward, and the "chair" is formed. The back is made by the loops held up by the right hand, the seat by the loop around the left thumb, and the four legs by the strings of the loops held by the left index and little finger (Fig. 15).

Fig. 15

"It was dark when he woke up, so he got a pair of scissors to cut off a candle."

Step Nine: Release the loop from the left thumb, and you have the "scissors" (Fig. 16).

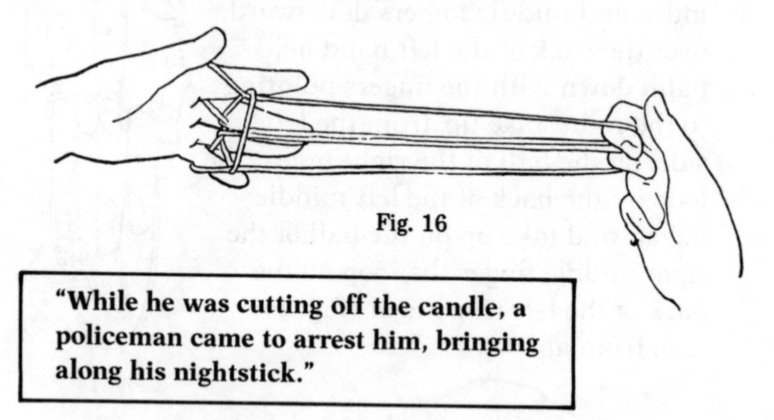

Fig. 16

"While he was cutting off the candle, a policeman came to arrest him, bringing along his nightstick."

Step Ten: Release the loop on the left index finger, and draw the hands gently apart to produce the long "nightstick," with the base at the end formed by the small crossed loops on the right index and middle finger (Fig. 17).

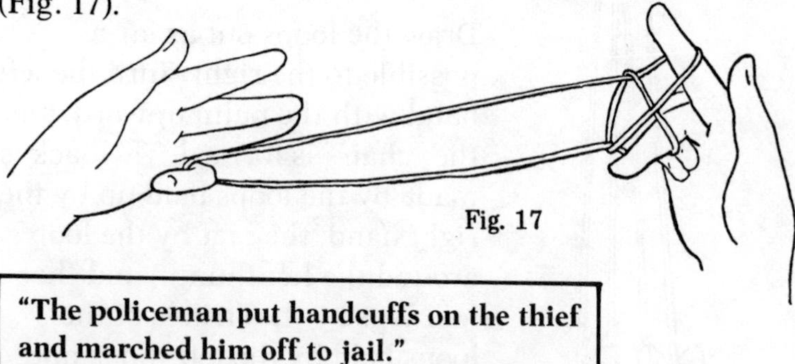

Fig. 17

"The policeman put handcuffs on the thief and marched him off to jail."

Step Eleven: Release the loop from the right index, and put the right hand through the right middle finger loop.

Put the left hand through the loop held by the left little finger. Separate the hands (Fig. 18) and draw the strings tight. This movement puts a loop on the left wrist and a slip noose on the right wrist—forming "handcuffs."

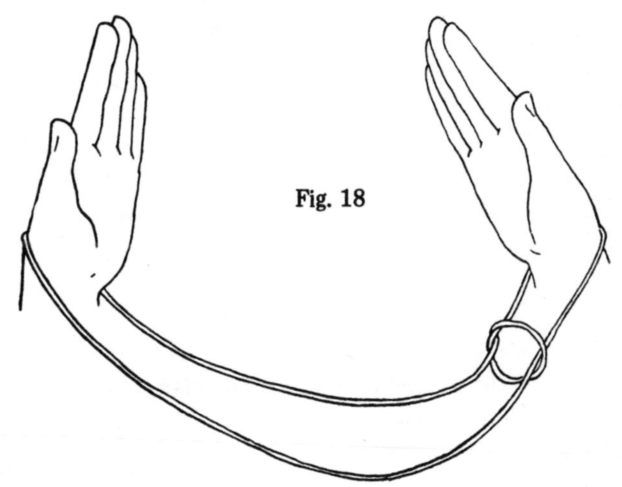

Fig. 18

A Man on a Bed

Step One: Opening A.

Step Two: Pass each thumb away from you under the index loop. Pick up, on the back of the thumb, the near little finger string, and return the thumb to its former position (Fig. 1).

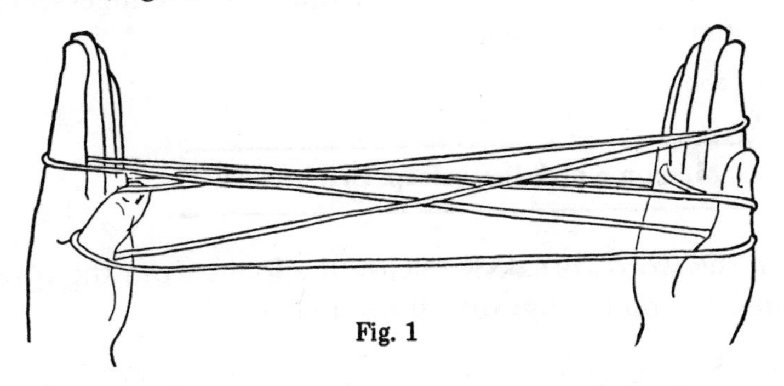

Fig. 1

Step Three: Pass each little finger toward you and, from above, through the index loop, pick up on the back of the little finger, the far thumb string (not the palmar string) (Fig. 2).

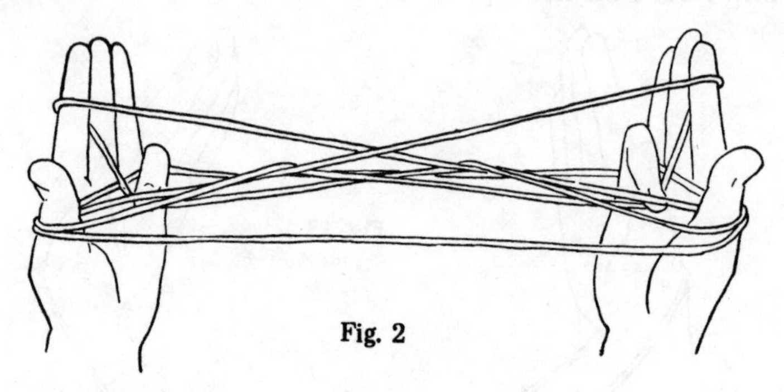

Fig. 2

Return the little finger to its position (Fig. 3).

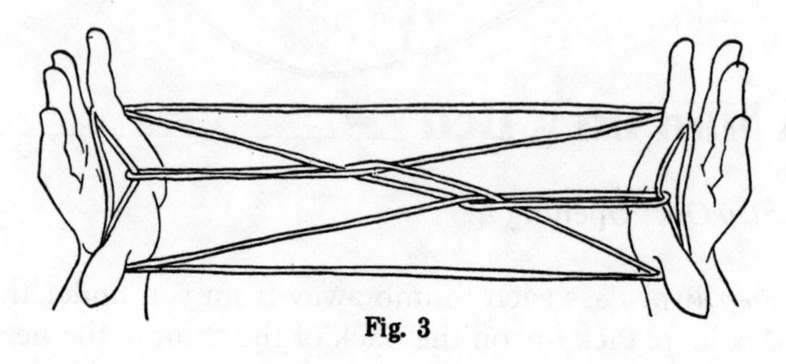

Fig. 3

Step Four: Release the loops from the index fingers, and the figure will appear.

Say:

Man on a bed, lies asleep. Bed breaks!

On the word "breaks," release the loops from the little fingers, and the figure will disappear!

6.
String Games

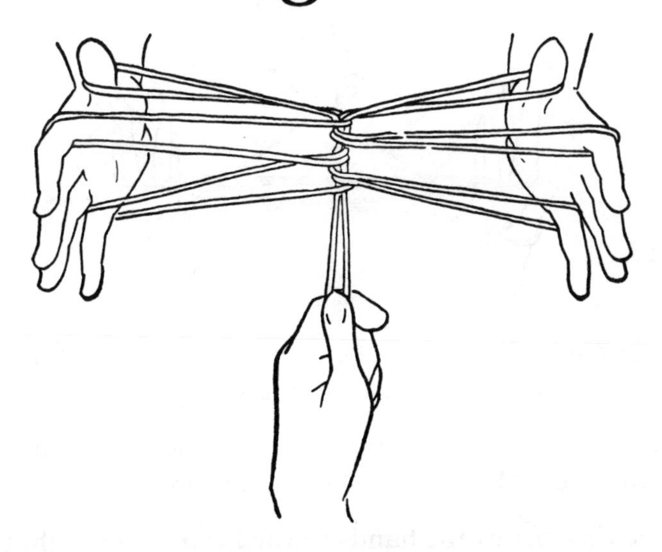

for Two

A Palm Tree
A Hut
A Six-Pointed Star
A House

A Palm Tree

Step One: Opening A.

Step Two: A second person, "A," catches the middle of the near thumb string and draws it away from you over all the other strings (Fig. 1).

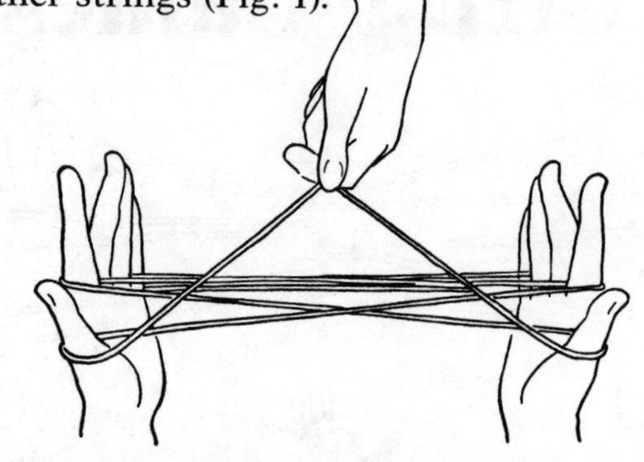

Fig. 1

Step Three: Exchange the loops on the little fingers, passing the right loop over the left loop.

Step Four: Exchange the loops on the index fingers, passing the right loop over the left loop.

Step Five: Draw the hands toward you to pull tight the loop held by "A". Work the strings to form the crown of the palm tree (Fig. 2).

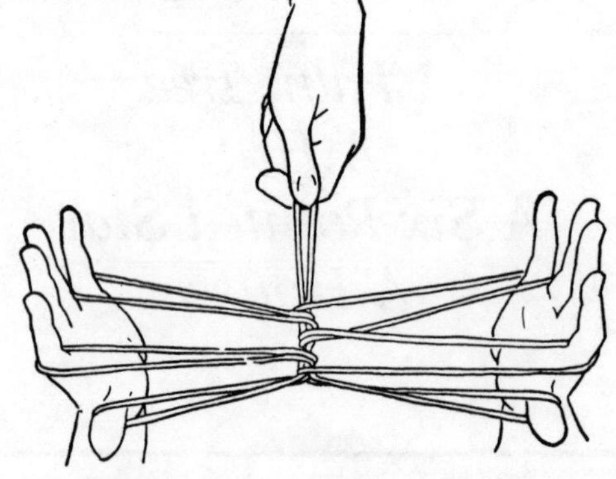

Fig. 2

A Hut

Step One: Put the untwisted loop on the index fingers only, and separate the hands. Pass each thumb from below into the index loop (Fig. 1, left hand). Bend it over the far index string and sweep it down, toward you, and up again (Fig. 1, right hand).

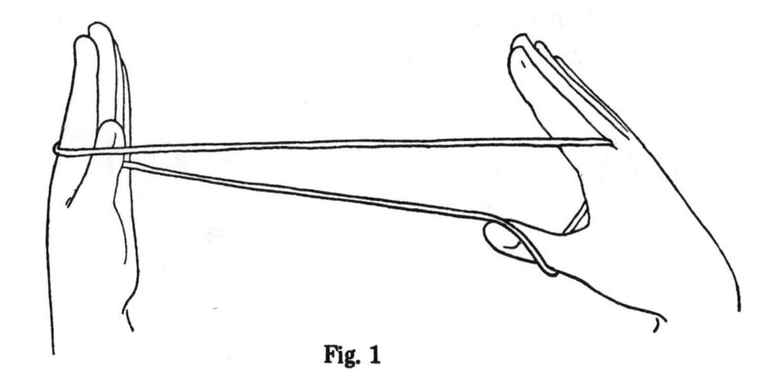

Fig. 1

In this way, you put crossed loops on the thumbs and index fingers (Fig. 2).

You now have, on each hand, a far thumb string and a near index string, and a palmar string passing from the near side of the thumb to the far side of the index.

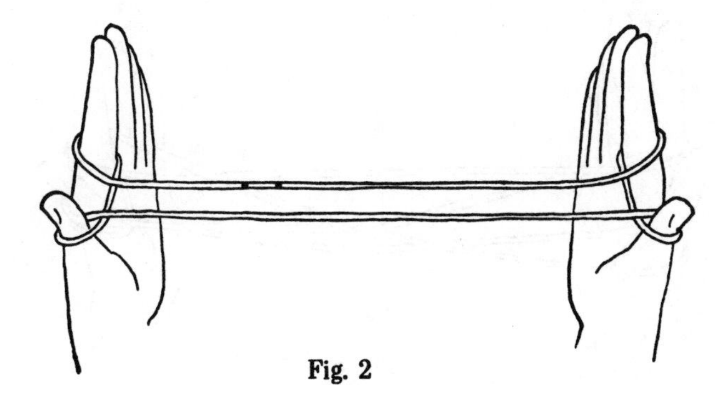

Fig. 2

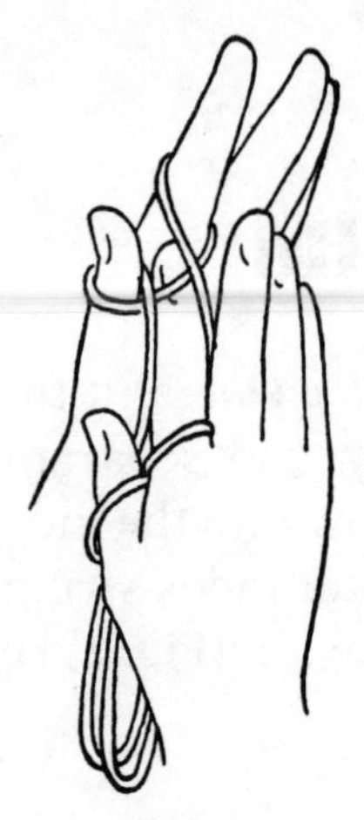
Fig. 3

Step Two: Put the right index from below under the left palmar string between the far thumb string and the near index string (Fig. 3). Draw the loop out on the back of the index, at the same time giving it one twist by rotating the index away from you, down, toward you, and up again (Fig. 4).

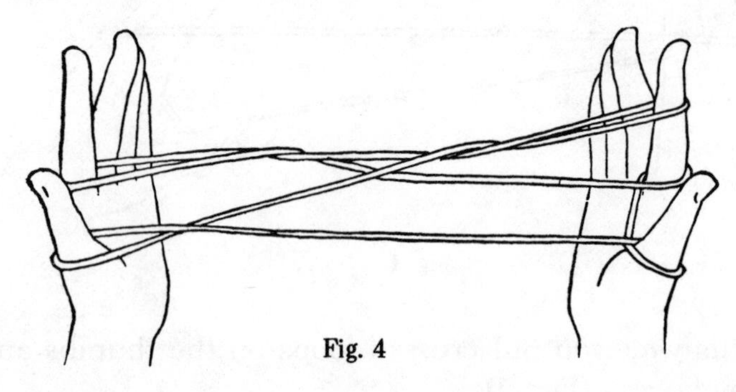
Fig. 4

Step Three: Put the right thumb from below into the right upper index loop. Separate the thumb from the index in order to make the loop wider (Fig. 5).

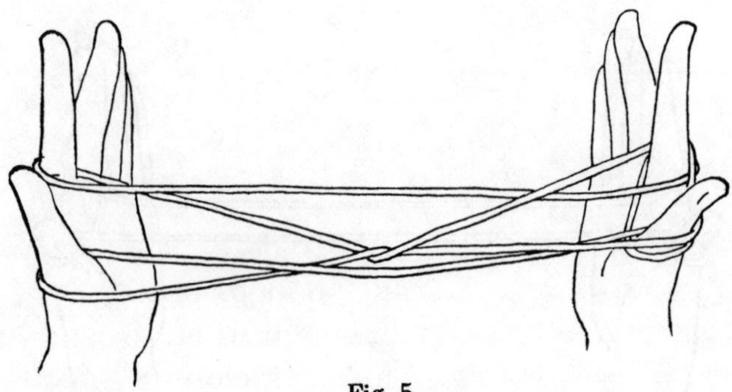
Fig. 5

Now pass the left index from above through this upper loop extended on the right thumb and index, and pick up, from below, (between the lower near index string and the lower far thumb string) on the back of the left index, the right palmar string (Fig. 6).

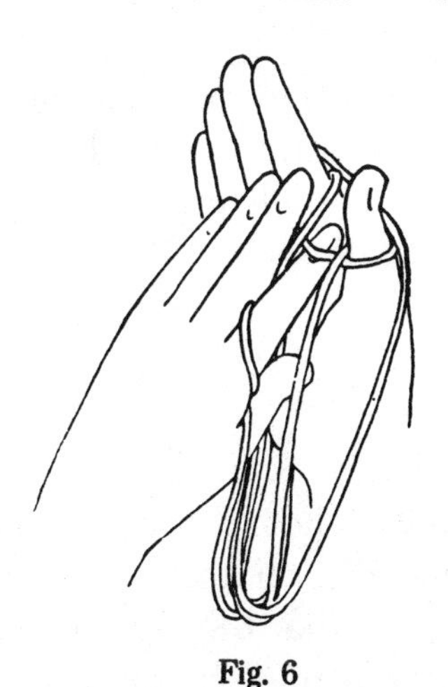

Fig. 6

Draw the loop out and give it one twist by rotating the left index away from you, down, toward you, and up again.

Step Four: Pass the left thumb from below into the upper left index loop. Separate the thumb from the index in order to make the loop wider (Fig. 7).

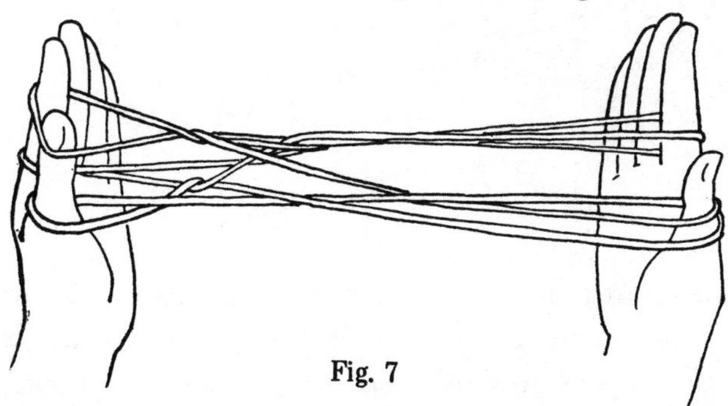

Fig. 7

Step Five: Bend the right middle, ring and little fingers toward you over all the loops on the right hand. Close these fingers on the palm to hold the strings in place while you gather together, close to the left hand, between the right thumb and index, all the loops on the left hand, by putting the right thumb below the loops and closing the right index down on them (Fig. 8).

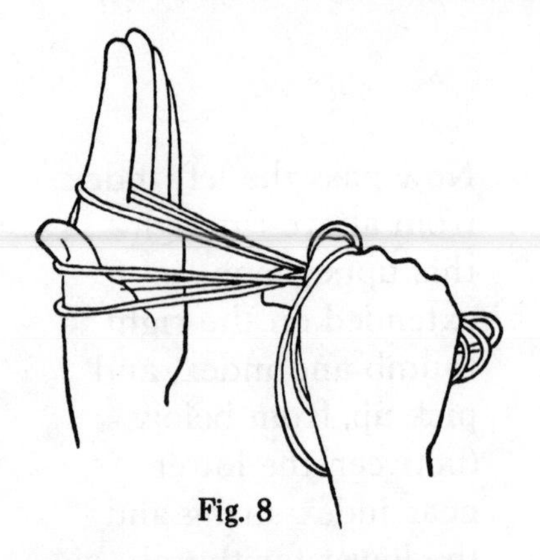

Fig. 8

Now withdraw the left hand from all the loops. With the right thumb and index, turn the loops over, away from you (so that the right thumb comes on top of the loops), and put the left thumb and index back into the loop, as they were before (Fig. 9), except: Now the left thumb loop goes on the left index; the left index loop goes on the left thumb and the loop common to both thumb and index is now the lower loop.

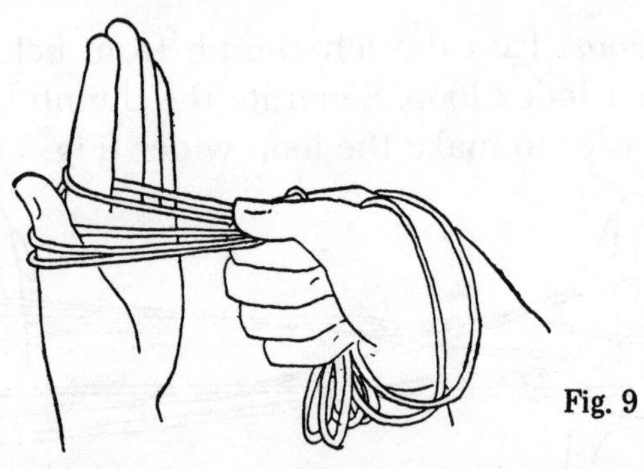

Fig. 9

Draw the hands apart and repeat the same movement on the right hand, as follows: Bend the left middle, ring and little fingers toward you over all the loops on the left hand. Close these fingers down on the palm to hold the strings in place while you gather together, with the left thumb and index, close to the right hand, all the loops on the left hand, putting the left thumb below the loops and closing the left index down on them. Now withdraw the right hand from all the loops. With the left thumb and index, turn the loops over, away from you (so that the left thumb comes on top of the loops). Put the right thumb and index back into the loops as they were before, except: Now the right thumb loop goes on the right index; the right index loop goes on the right thumb; and the loop common to both right thumb and index is now the lower loop. Separate the hands and draw the strings tight (Fig. 10).

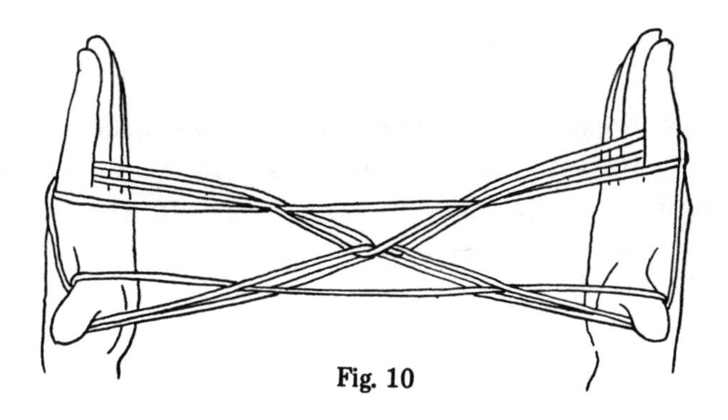

Fig. 10

The figure now consists of an upper string, which is a single straight near index string passing on either side between the two far index strings; a lower string, which is a single straight far thumb string passing, on each side, between the two near thumb strings; and double near thumb and far index strings twisted together in the center.

Step Six: The second person now pulls upward the twisted strings in the center of the figure, while you bend each index down toward you, over the near index string, and each thumb away from you over the far thumb string (Fig. 11).

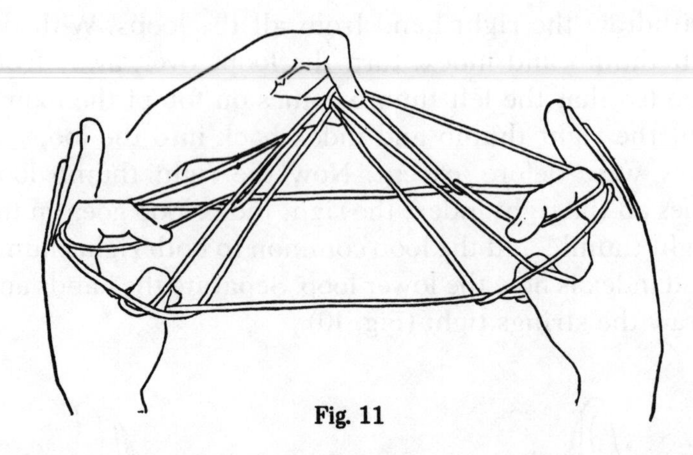

Fig. 11

Holding these strings down, you let the other strings slip off the thumbs and index fingers. Now turn the hands with the palms down, and separate the thumbs widely from the index fingers, and the "hut" is formed (Fig. 12).

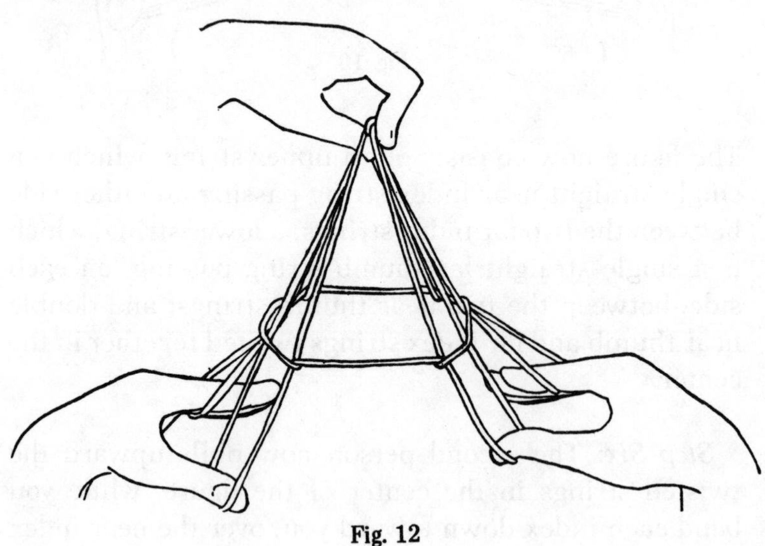

Fig. 12

A Six-Pointed Star

Step One: Form "A Hut."

Step Two: The second person releases the loops he has been holding up, and pulls out in opposite directions the straight strings at the sides of the figure (Fig. 1).

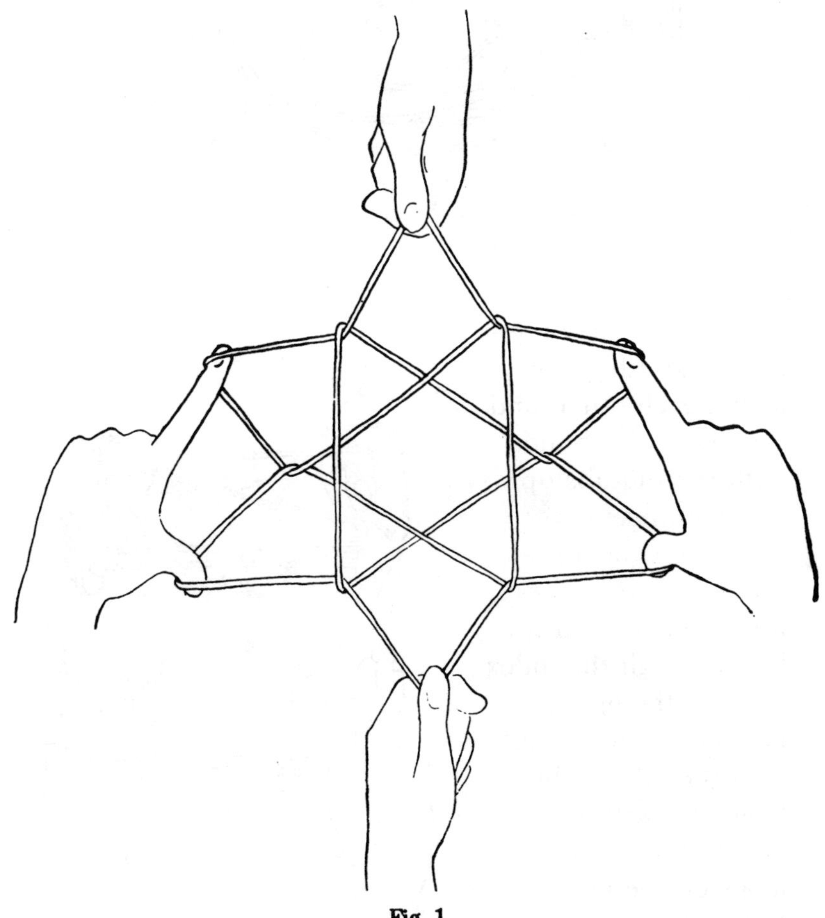

Fig. 1

A House

Step One: Two players (A and B) each take a loop of string and form Opening A.

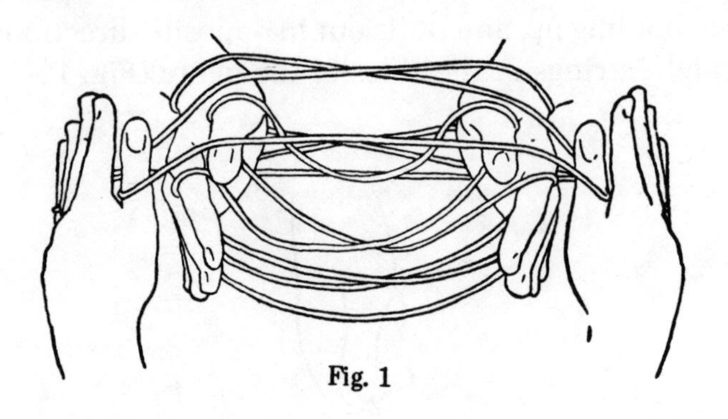

Fig. 1

Step Two: They then stand close together facing each other, and each turns his hands with the thumbs up and the fingers directed toward the other. Then A passes his hands away from him through the index loops of the figure held on the hands of B. B then draws his hands toward him, but leaves his index loops on the wrists of A (Fig. 1, Fig. 2).

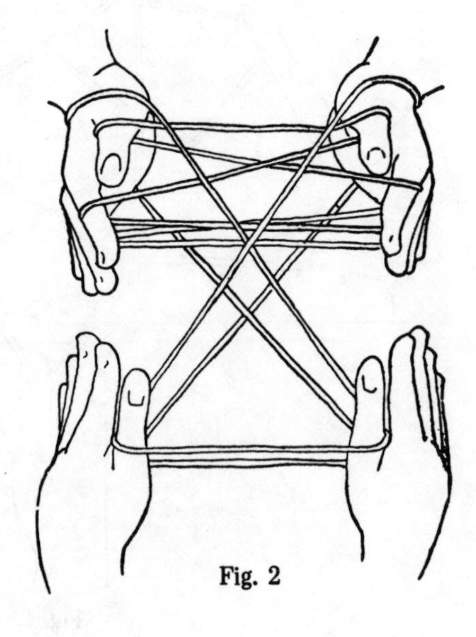

Fig. 2

Step Three: B passes his hands away from him through the index loops of the figure held on the hands of A. A draws his hands toward him, but leaves his index loops on the wrists of B (Fig. 3).

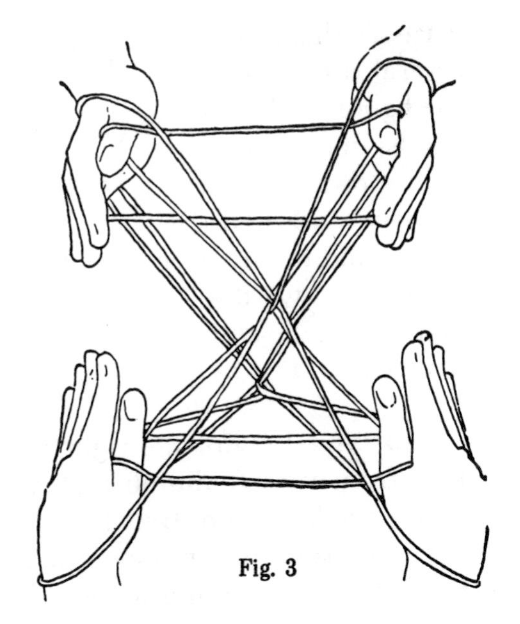

Fig. 3

Step Four: A now takes his hands entirely out of the figure that he has been holding. Gathering together all the strings running to B's hands, A straightens them and then twists them into a rope (Fig. 4).

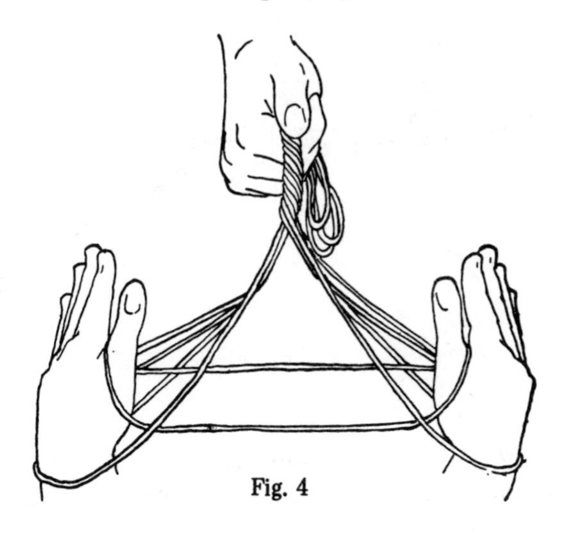

Fig. 4

A Passes this rope several times around the figure held in B's hands, under the figure toward B, then up between B and the figure, and finally over the figure toward A, and allows the end to hang down (Fig. 5).

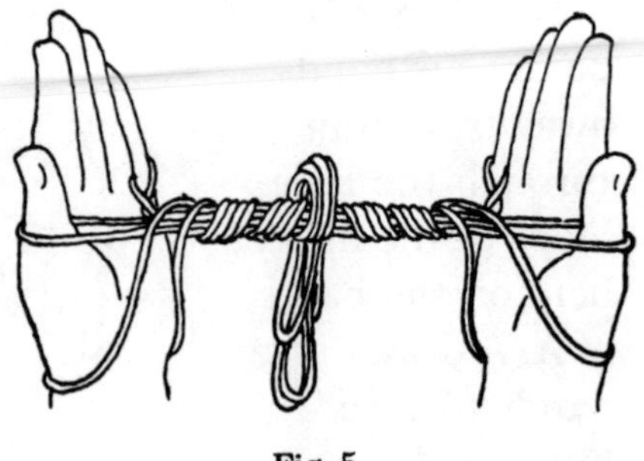

Fig. 5

Step Five: A, with the right hand, now removes the loop from B's left thumb and, with the left hand, removes the loop from B's left little finger. B removes his left hand from the wrist loop, and picks up, with the left hand, the right thumb loop and the right little finger loop. B removes his right hand from the wrist loop, and then transfers, to his right hand, the right little finger loop (Fig. 6).

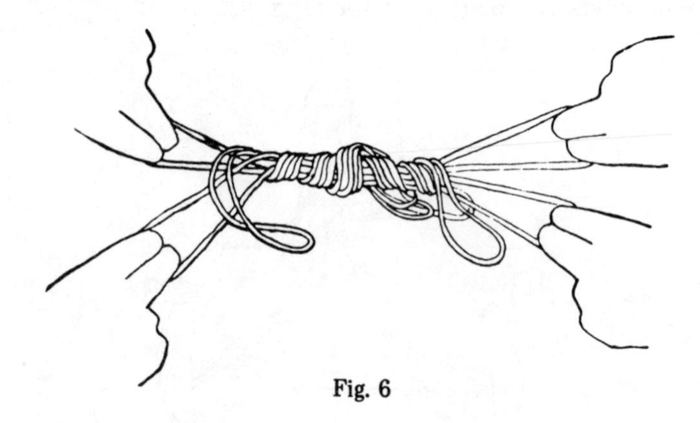

Fig. 6

A and B now draw the hands apart, working the figure until the large square pattern appears (Fig. 7).

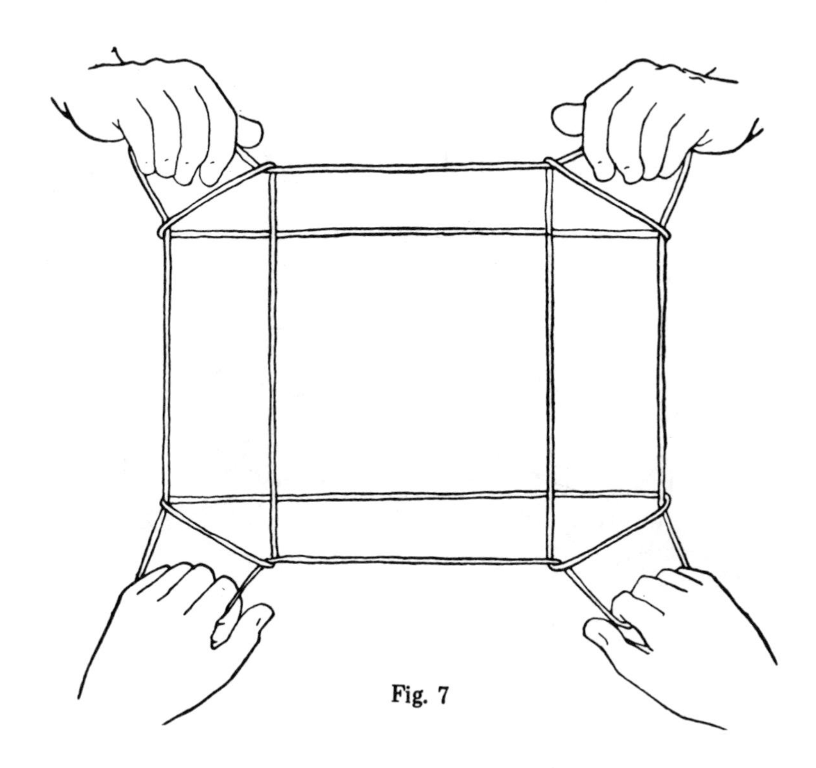

Fig. 7

Step Six: A and B now sit down opposite each other, crossing their legs and drawing up their knees. Each places the loop held by the right hand on the left foot, and the loop held by the left hand on the right foot. The feet must be pressed down firmly to keep the loops secure. A now brings together the pair of inner strings that pass at right angles under the other pair of inner strings, and with both hands, lifts them up to form the top beam of the "house" (See Fig. 8 on next page).

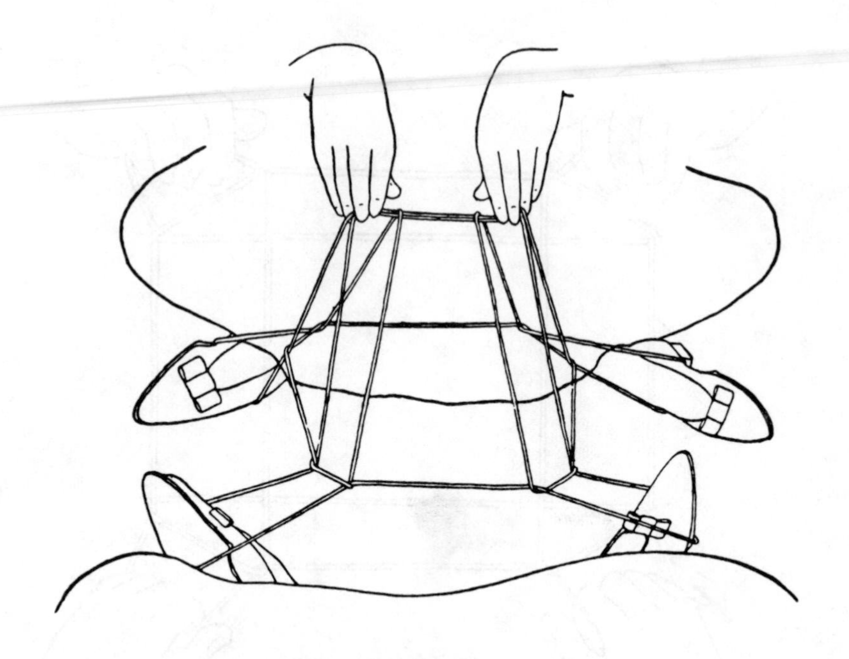

Fig. 8

7. Cat's Cradle

The Cradle
A Soldier's Bed
Candles
A Manger
Diamonds
Cat's Eye
Fish in a Dish
Grandfather Clock

Cat's Cradle, the most familiar of all string games, is well known in China, Korea, Japan, the Philippines and Borneo. It is believed to have begun in these Asian countries and spread throughout Europe and North America.

You need two people and one loop of string. You play by taking turns removing the string from each other's hands to produce eight definite designs.

In the following description, we'll call the players A and B. The terms "near," "far," "right," and "left" refer to the position of the strings as seen by the person from whose hands the figure is being taken.

THE CRADLE

Step One: A takes the string, passes the four fingers of each hand through the untwisted loop, and separates the hands.

Then, with the thumb and index of the right hand, he turns the left near string away from him across the left palm, and then toward him across the back of the left hand, bringing the string to the right between the left thumb and index.

In the same way, he turns the right near string once around the right hand.

There are now two strings across the back of each hand and a single string across each palm.

Step Two: Opening A, but pick up the palmar string with the middle finger instead of the index.

There is now a loop on each middle finger and two strings across the back of each hand. The "cradle" is formed by a straight near string, a straight far string, and the crossed strings of the middle finger loops (Fig. 1).

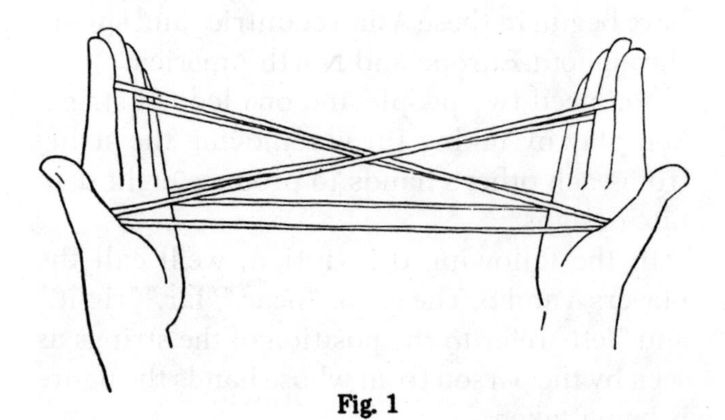

Fig. 1

A SOLDIER'S BED

B puts his left thumb away from A under the right near middle finger string and his left index away from A under the left near middle finger string. Then, by bringing the thumb and index together, B picks up, between their tips, the two near middle finger strings just where they cross at the near side of the figure.

In the same way, he picks up the two far middle finger strings, by putting the right thumb toward A under the right far middle finger string, and the right index toward A under the left far middle finger string. Then B brings thumb and index together to hold the two strings where they cross at the far side of the figure (Fig. 2).

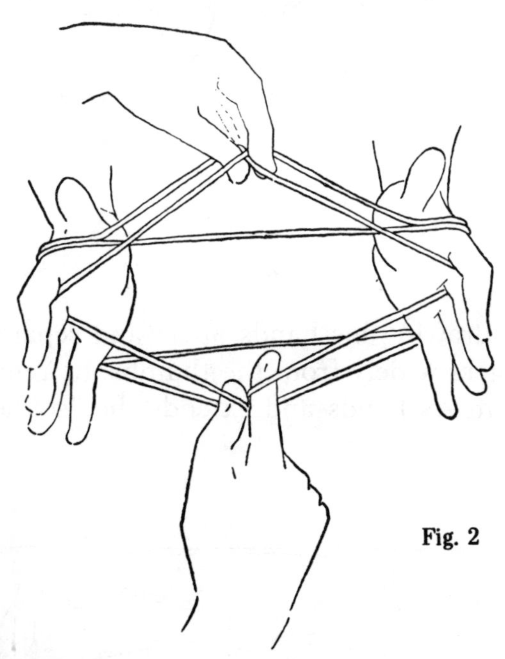

Fig. 2

Now B separates the hands. Drawing the right hand away from A and the left hand toward A, he carries the thumb and index of each hand, still holding the strings, around the corresponding side string of the figure and up into the center of the figure (Fig. 3).

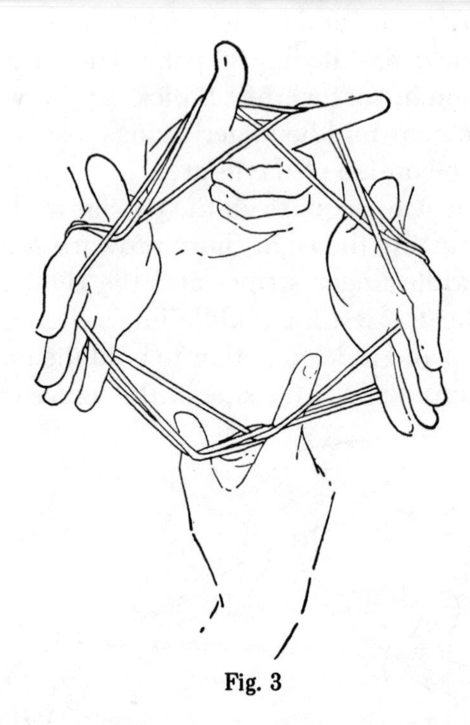

Fig. 3

Then, by drawing his hands apart and separating the index fingers widely from the thumbs, he removes the figure from A's hands and extends the "soldier's bed" (Fig. 4).

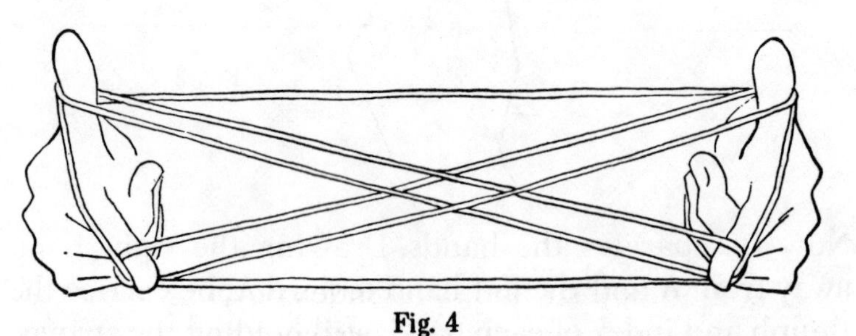

Fig. 4

CANDLES

A inserts his left index, from above, into the left thumb loop, near the center of the figure, and his left thumb, from above, into the right thumb loop. Then, bringing thumb and index together, he picks up between their tips the near thumb strings just where they cross.

In the same way, by inserting the right thumb from above into the right index loop and the right index from above into the left index loop, A picks up the two far index strings where they cross.

A then separates the hands—drawing the right hand away from B over, and past, the far straight string—and the left hand toward B over, and past, the near straight string (Fig. 5).

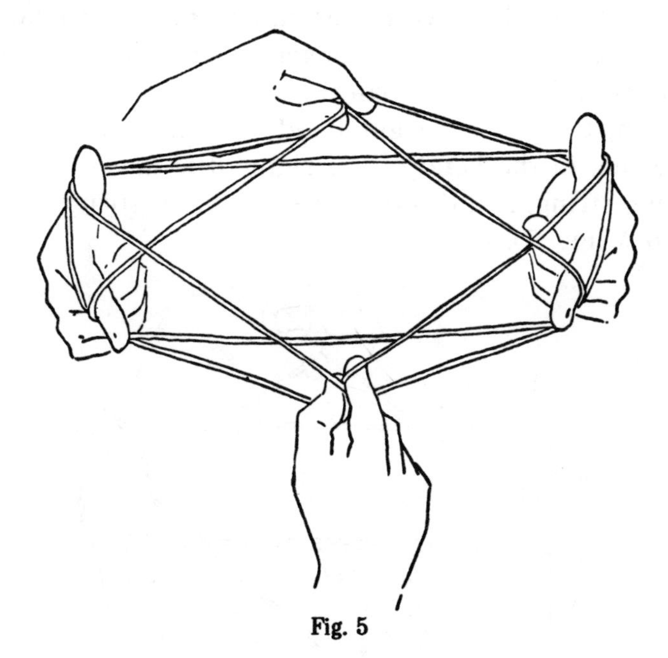

Fig. 5

Finally, he puts the thumb and index of each hand (still holding the strings) under the corresponding side string and from below into the center of the figure. Then, by drawing the hands apart and separating the index fingers widely from the thumbs, he takes the figure from B's hands (Fig. 6).

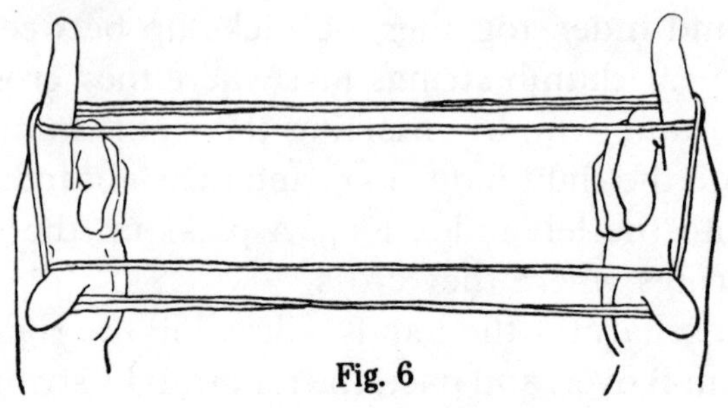

Fig. 6

A MANGER

B turns his left hand with the palm facing upward, takes up in the bend of the little finger, the near index string, and draws it over the strings toward A.

Then, turning his right hand with the palm up, B takes up, in the bend of the right little finger, the far thumb string, and draws it over the other strings away from A (Fig. 7).

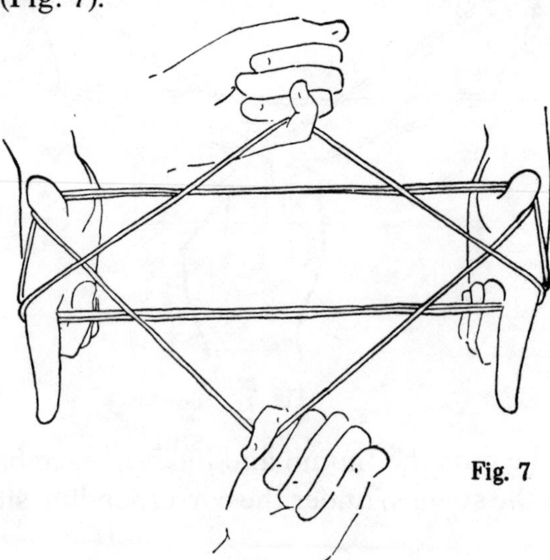

Fig. 7

Closing the little fingers on the palms, he passes the left thumb and index from the near side under the two near thumb strings and up on the far side of them. At the same time, B passes the right thumb and index from the far side under the two far index strings and up on the near side of them (Fig. 8).

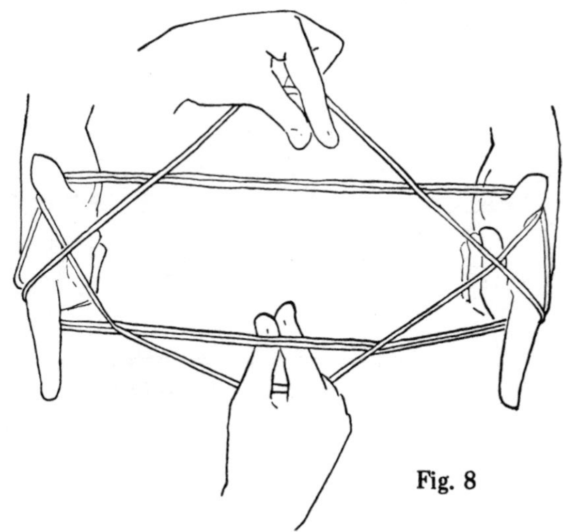

Fig. 8

Then, drawing the hands apart, and separating the index fingers widely from the thumbs, he takes the figure from A's hands (Fig. 9).

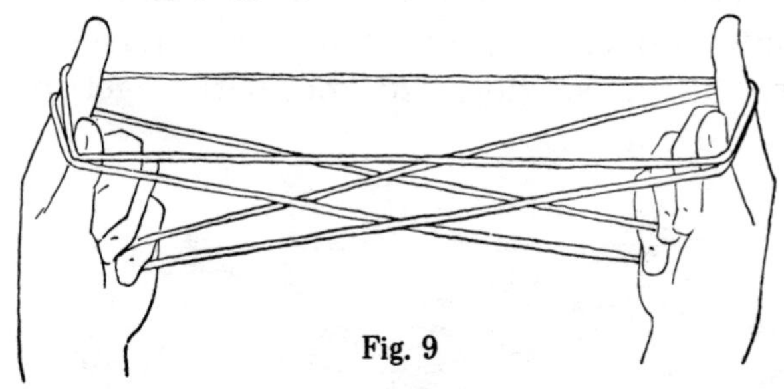

Fig. 9

He now has two strings passing across the backs of the thumb and index of each hand and a loop held to the palm by each little finger.

DIAMONDS

A now takes the "manger" from B's hands in the same way that B took the cradle from his hands, but the thumb and index of each hand (holding between their tips the two crossed strings) are brought up around the corresponding side string and down into the center of the figure (Fig. 10).

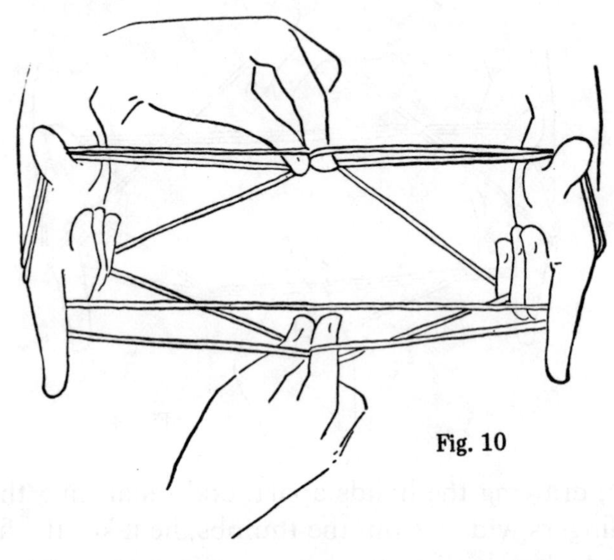

Fig. 10

Then, when the hands are drawn apart, and the thumbs and index fingers widely separated, A forms a figure exactly like the "soldier's bed," but with fingers pointing downward (Fig. 11).

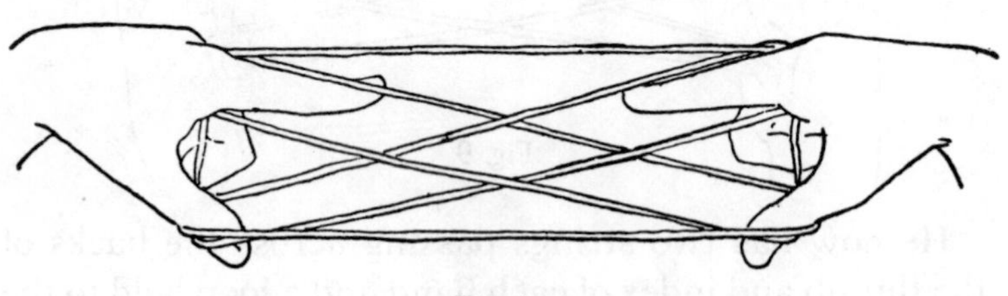

Fig. 11

CAT'S EYE

B takes the figure from A's hand in the same way that A took the "soldier's bed" from B to form the "candles" (Fig. 12), pinching the crossed strings between the thumb and index fingers, and pulling them out, around and up into the center of the figure.

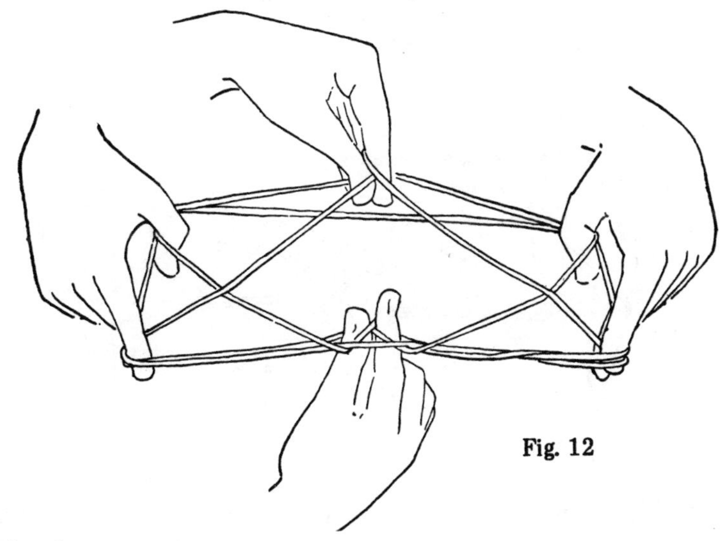

Fig. 12

The figure is finally extended between the thumb and index widely separated (Fig. 13).

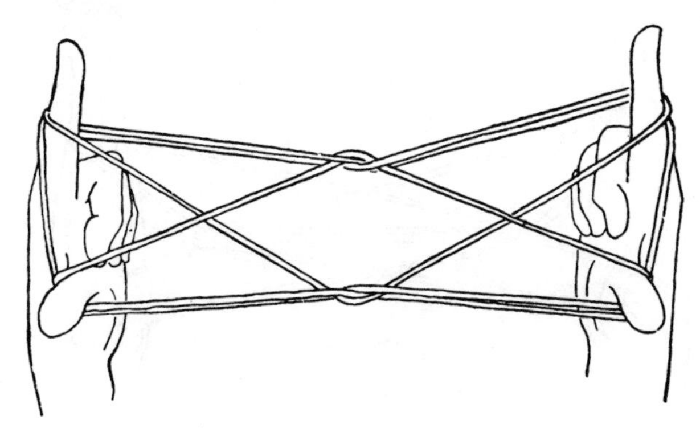

Fig. 13

FISH IN A DISH

A inserts the right index from above into the far left triangle, and his right thumb from above into the far right triangle. He puts his left index from above into the near left triangle and his left thumb from above into the near right triangle. He turns the thumbs and index fingers up (Fig. 14).

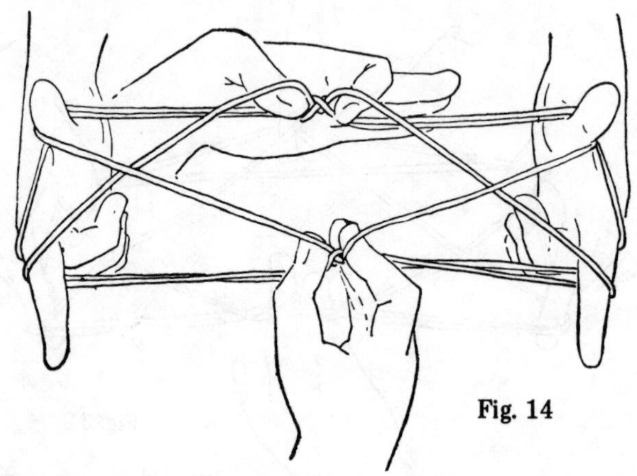

Fig. 14

Then he draws his hands apart, separates the index fingers widely from the thumbs, and takes the figure from B's hands (Fig. 15).

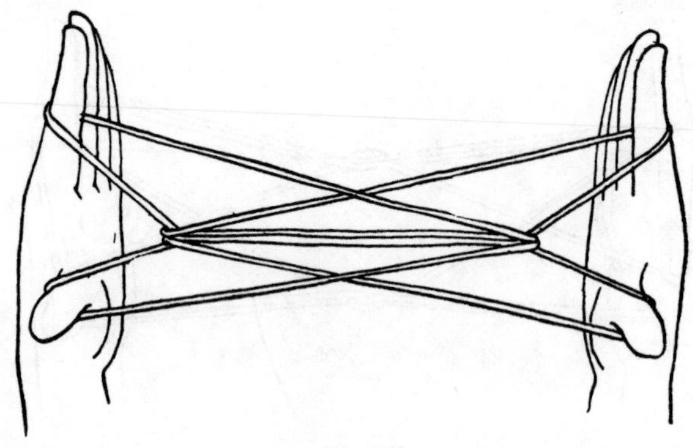

Fig. 15

GRANDFATHER CLOCK

Step One: B arranges the two strings that pass from side to side through the center of "fish in a dish" so that, uncrossed, they can easily be separated into a near string and a far string.

Step Two: B now turns his left palm upward, and picks up, in the bend of the left little finger, the *near* string that passes through the center of the figure, drawing it over the other strings toward A.

Then, turning the right hand with the palm facing upward, he picks up, in the bend of the right little finger the *far* string that passes through the center of the figure, drawing it over the other strings away from A (Fig. 16).

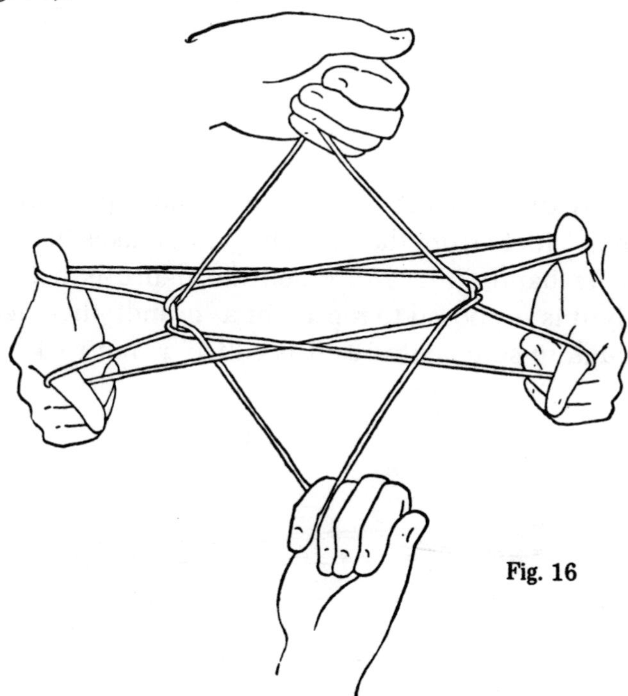

Fig. 16

Putting the right thumb from above into the right far triangle, the right index from above into the left far triangle, the left thumb from above into the right near triangle, and the left index from above into the left near triangle, B turns the thumb and index of each hand toward the center of the figure and up into the center (Fig. 17).

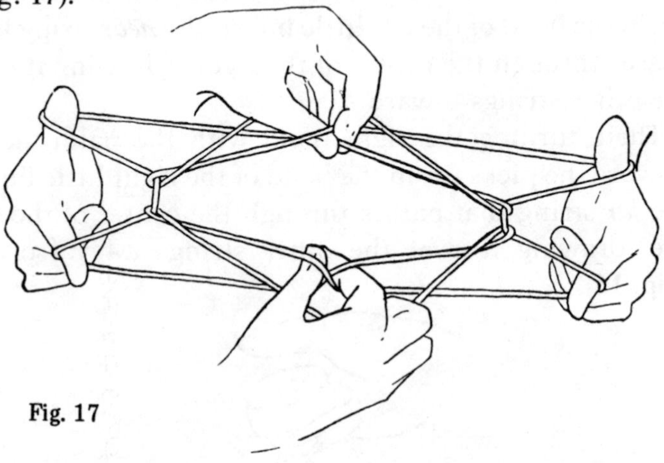

Fig. 17

Then, by drawing the hands apart, and separating the thumbs widely from the index fingers, B takes the figure from A's hands (Fig. 18). When the figure is held vertically, it is supposed to represent a "grandfather clock," although in some cultures it is called a "hat rack."

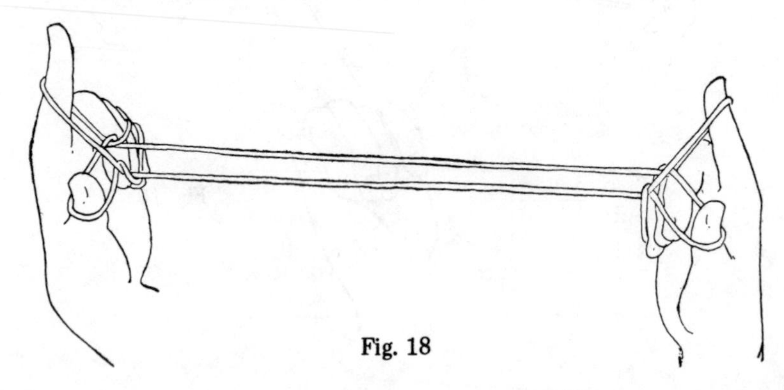

Fig. 18

String Games Chart and Index

Game	Page	Discovered in	Other Names (Tribe)
Apache Door	44	U.S.–Ariz. –N.M.	A poncho (Navajo) A sling (Zuni, Apache)
Big Star	36	U.S.–N.M.	(Navajo)
Bow	74	U.S.–Ariz.	(Navajo)
Broom	38	U.K.	
Candle Caper	92	U.K.	Tallow Dips
Candles	119	see *Cat's Cradle*	Chopsticks (Korea) Mirror (Denmark)
Casting a Spear	58	Torres Straits (Pacific) Canada (B.C.)	A Fish Spear Pitching a Tent Sea-Egg Spear
Cat's Cradle	115	Worldwide	Well Rope (China) Woof-taking (Korea) Witch's Game (Germany) The Saw (France)
Cat's Eye	123	see *Cat's Cradle*	Cow's Eyeball (Korea) Horse's Eye (Japan) Diamonds (U.K.)
Circle	14	Canada	*Ussuqdjung* (Eskimo)
Cradle	116	see *Cat's Cradle*	Hearse Cover (Korea)
Diamonds	122	see *Cat's Cradle*	Soldier's Bed Again (U.K.)
Dogs on a Leash	22	U.K.	Leashing of Lochiel's Dogs Tying Dogs' Feet (Scotland) Duck's Feet (Ireland)
		France	Cock's Feet (Algeria)
		U.S.	Crow's Feet (Cherokee, Onandagas, Tananas of Alaska)
		Australia	4-Pronged Spear
		East Africa	Wooden Spoon
Fighting Headhunters	50	Torres Straits (Pacific)	Murray & Dauar Men Fighting
Fish in a Dish	124	see *Cat's Cradle*	Rice Mill Pestle (Korea)
Full & Empty Well	70	Torres Straits (Pacific)	Nest of the Ti Bird A Canoe
Grandfather Clock	125	see *Cat's Cradle*	Hat Rack

STRING GAMES CHART AND INDEX

Game	Page	Discovered in	Other Names (Tribe)
House	110	W. Carolines Australia U.S.–Okla.	(UAP) (Aborigines) (Osage)
Hut	103	U.S.–N.M. –Ore. –N.M.	(Pueblo) (Klamath) Brush House (Zuni)
Jacob's Ladder	26	U.S.–Okla. –Hawaii Ireland	(Osage) *Ma-ka-lii-lii-* or *Pu-kau-la* The Ladder or the Fence
Letter M– and Letter W	16	U.S.–Virginia	(Omaha)
Lizard	78	U.S.–Ariz.	(Navajo)
Magic Carpet	19	U.S.–Ariz. –N.M.	Carrying Wood (Zuni)
Man on a Bed	99	Torres Straits	
Manger	120	see *Cat's Cradle*	Upside Down Cradle (U.K.)
Many Stars	32	U.S.–Ariz. –N.M.	(Navajo)
North Star	37	U.S.–Ariz.	Big Star (Navajo)
Palm Tree	102	Torres Straits	(U)
Rabbit	81	U.S.–Ore.	(Klamath)
Rising & Setting Sun	85	U.S.–Ore.	(Klamath)
Setting Sun	54	Torres Straits	Star
Six-Pointed Star	109	U.S.–N.M. –Okla.	Star (Pueblo) (Klamath)
Slithering Sea Serpent	60	Torres Straits (Pacific)	Sea Snake
Soldier's Bed	117	see *Cat's Cradle*	Chessboard (Korea) Mountain Cat (Japan) Church Window (U.K.) Fish Pond (U.S.) Scissors (France)
Tent	88	U.S.–Ariz.	(Navajo)
Three Diamonds	65	Torres Straits (Pacific)	Kingfish Sea-Cow
Two Coyotes	39	U.S.–Ariz.	(Navajo)